I0690079

TRANSHUMANCE

TRANSHUMANCE

ANDREW F. GILES

New Orleans & New York

Published in the United States of America by
Queer Space
A Rebel Satori Imprint
www.rebelsatoripress.com

Copyright © 2025 by Andrew F. Giles

ALL RIGHTS RESERVED. Except for brief passages quoted in newspaper, magazine, radio, television, or online reviews, no part of this book may be reproduced in any form or any means, electronic or mechanical, including photocopying, recording, or information or retrieval system, without the permission in writing from the publisher. Please do not participate in or encourage piracy of copyrighted materials in violation of the author's rights. Purchase only authorized editions.

This is a work of fiction. Names, characters, places, and incidents are the product of the author's imagination and are used fictitiously and any resemblance to actual persons, living or dead, business establishments, events, or locales is entirely coincidental. The publisher does not have any control over and does not assume any responsibility for author or third-party websites or their content.

Title font: Broadstreet copyright © Three Islands Press.

Paperback ISBN: 978-1-60864-386-8

We must be on some mountain-top at night,
with a full moon riding the black above
but tongues and limbs of mist stretching below,
mist or cloud we can hardly be sure,
cloud or sea we can hardly be sure[1]

Shortened adaptations or extracts of work from this novella appear as 'Transhumance' in *The Selkie* (2023) and 'Stewards' in *Queer Life, Queer Love* (Muswell Press, 2021)

PART I

CHAPTER 1: EVERYTHING

The outside is not coming in this year, he thought, heaving the drainpipe back into place against the wind and tying it tight with string. Everything was steady. The pipe rattling against the buffeting gale. The trees screeching, leaves and branches ripped from their bodies. Everything will be used.

Warming the man and his dogs, alive behind its window, stood the tube burner. The fire was like everything else: vital, with its own unquantifiable, uncontrollable spirit. His two dogs slept on, ready for the man to move, when they would slip into jealous circling and mutterings of food. A storm had attacked the mountain since the last crisp bright day had suddenly clouded over at dusk. I'm tired lads, he said. The mastiff nudged his big head over to the man's knee, jowls in deep folds, brown eyes cadogan. He scratched the big dog under the chin, then jumped as a crack sounded outside. There was always something to stop the man in his tracks. What about the sparks when he put the plug in? The little mongrel dug his way under the blankets as hail clattered against the window. A voice sung its cave charm in the limestone peaks—*everyone calm*.

A nearby owl hooted into the squall. Torn out of its chest by the wind, the hollow sound as soon disappeared, grabbed by the night. The man's little world was barely sealed. His cabin was covered in a curved, shimmering orb, with mesh-like skin that let the cherry wood smoke out. But what was being let out, and what was being let in? This tiny universe was a breathing lung, edged with ferns, and the bristle of holly. The mastiff suddenly leapt up and bayed at the night, making the little dog jump under his blanket. There was usually something at the edge of the mastiff's hearing—a wild pig, the bear, a distant wolf howling. Will you go out, dog? asked the man. The mastiff stood at the door growling with his tail high. The fire spat and swore behind its glass door. I'll let you out, idiot. You stay here, rat, he nodded to the little one, whose head was peering from under the blanket. The mastiff charged out of the door into the storm, bark high and loud, tiger coat on end. Everything is safe.

Pretty quiet today, he grinned at the little dog. Not helicopter or wolf pack or jalopy in sight. Outside the broken-skinned orb of his mountain cabin, the world was wrecked and hurricane-blasted. What a hullabaloo, he shouted to the mastiff who hackled and roared against the wind, just outside the door. Good dog, fine dog. What were the trees saying, now that the wind was laying them out horizontal? He watched them, fingertips tingling. Some gripped with their roots, hooting messages out across the mountainside. The holly, strongest little tree in a storm, was the reassuring broker of calm amongst the babbling underground network: Temperate-feel. Moss-bung. Light-in-the-burrows. Storm-dance. They created composite actions from single notes. The ash, long and thin, understood how parts of the grid would break up. The man would thank them for it as he gathered scattered branches for kindling. The elder, a witch that flowed and shunted into the wind, and was shaped by it, wiggled their fingers in signs. The man shivered along his tattooed arms. The network is bristling, my friends, screamed a herd of shadow-shifting oak across the system. The mastiff heard them, too, and stood strong against the wind as it spun around the house-orb and ruffled the enormous herds of trees, miles across. The wolf watched it all from her vantage point. Everything is alive, she whispered.

The man woke, feeling stiffness in his arms and legs, pinned for a moment to the forest floor under six blankets. Morning rat, he said to the little dog, who jumped up and skittled his paws across the floor, shook his head furiously, ears tapping against his face, before stretching in downward dog and yawning wide. Sleep well? The dog trotted off. Fair enough, rat. Where's your big brother? The little dog barked *food*. The man hauled himself out of bed, groaning, walked to the front door and opened it. Survive the night, beast? He looked down at the huge mastiff, curled up in an arc like a baby. He's still asleep, rat. The little dog trotted over and nudged the mastiff, whose head shot up with a start. Morning beast. Let's get down the field. Both dogs were immediately awake, ready to shoot down the stairs to the gate. Wait a minute you two, I haven't got my outside feet on yet. I don't have a hairy outdoor coat like yours. Useless, said the dogs. They gazed at him expectantly as he put his boots on, pulled another jumper over the first, a coat, gloves, scarf, scraped his greasy hair back and took the keys to the barn off their hook. Right, let's go. The orb had opened out overnight and birdsong flooded in. Mist curled around the high mountain valley, settling on the never-green. As promised, the ash tree had left parts of itself strewn across the ground. The man bowed his head. The mastiff ran up to the neighbour's field. She looked at him over the fence, eyes glazed in liquid crystal display. None of the words she used were ones that he knew. The man waved, wishing the orb whole again. Come on beast, he muttered. Everything is protected.

CHAPTER 2: THE TIME OF SNOW

The man remembered the time of snow. He'd trudged along tarnie paths cut through walls of ice a metre high to get to the barn. The chickens leapt at him, wings noisy as he fed them, little dinosaurs. Another time, high in the mountain pastures, he'd come across a big pile of bones—jawbones, thigh, leg—wedged into a gully. The dogs spent some time inspecting them. At first, he'd presumed it was a wolf kill, and called the dogs closer, in case there was a den nearby. Then, later, as he walked back down the old drover's path and on to the tarmac road that was rugged with potholes, he met his neighbour, the hippy. Others called him the sheep-herd, though he had no sheep. But his father had. Was that a wolf kill, do you think? No, that was a group of donkeys (the mountain folk at times called horses 'donkeys') fucked by the snow. And the man supposed he was right. How's life down the mountain, he asked. There was a bear cub at the corner of the road, mate, by the headquarters of the guard. That's close to town, don't you think? Times are changing, too many bears, not enough work, laughed the hippy, eyes twinkling. You're in a good mood, hippy. Aye, so would you be if someone gave you a massive rail of coke at eleven o' clock in the morning. Nice, said the man. Well, that's it, I'm off to the cabin. Me, too, said the man, and they parted ways. The hippy disappeared in a cloud of ice and dust, up into the mountain in his old jalopy with tinted windows. Rush hour, the man said to the dogs. The mastiff lay in the snow, waiting to move on. The little dog pricked his ears, always listening to whatever the man had to say. That's right rat, he's gone, all coked up in the snow.

The town was about two thousand feet down the mountain. It was unwelcoming, geographically protected from outside attack, and still had one or two shops, usually with half-empty shelves. This was the time of emergencies and data tribes and post-war and price hikes. It felt, in the man's innards, as if the town had been dropped many miles below at the bottom of a precipice. Who dropped it? asked the dogs. Dunno; just feels like that. Other things seemed not quite right about the town. Townsfolk considered the world with shipwrecked expressions, mumbling worriedly under their breath. The horses gathered at the gates of their fields with their ears back. A single dog, teeth bared but tail wagging, walked up and down the centre of the high street. There were beautiful things too. A tiny bar with an ancient, cobbled floor that only served cold young red wine and fried chunks of bacon on yesterday's bread, toasted. Two men who held hands in the field as they tended to their donkeys. A storm had collapsed the delicate arc of stone that, millions of years ago, flung itself over the thin entrance to valley where the town had been dropped. But by who? We were there, said the voice from the cave. The shaman who flung it was a man dressed in the skin of a woman. It was still hard to leave and return. The townspeople asked, what was getting in and what was getting out? Some people claimed to know exactly what squeezed or drove or clambered over the crumbled rock, and many said the bear stood high above the pass, watching. The man didn't know. He peered at the town from high above, the bear sapiens. The voice from the caves sung of the hare and the roe deer and the wild horse, of a man who moved on in the middle of the night, called by his ancestors into the karst system. Which of the gods told you this? How did the snow enter the mountain pass? Then an enormous block of ice had become dislodged from the roof and smashed through his internet antenna.

He slipped and slid his way down the mountain to the town and knocked on the door of the council's computer pod, which had two very slow computers that sometimes ventured online. The council person answered the door. Hi, said the man, can I use the internet? Yeah sure, answered the council person, have you just come down the mountain in this weather? I had my ski poles, offered the man. Oh, right, OK—well, help yourself. The man sat at a computer and opened the browser. He searched "end of the world" and many millions of options appeared. He clicked on the second one, *when will the world end? Meteors are awesome to watch*, it stated, *and completely harmless*. The man sat for a moment more. There was an insect on the screen, making a trail from the bottom of the screen straight up to the top. Have you found what you needed? I think so, he said. He closed the window, stood up, and walked to the door. Thank-you, he said. The council person looked him up and down. Take it steady, they responded, their voice faraway. As the man left the council pod, the council person ran behind him, brandishing ski poles. Your ski poles! Oh, thanks. The man climbed back up the mountain in the dark, his head torch picking out eyes on the edges of the old ways. His heart beat quickly, the cold dove into his lungs. The mountain was protected by a huge glittering skull of stars and satellites that beetled across the bone. He put his fingers up to the edge of the skull, feeling the cold material. A voice travelled to him out of the darkness, but the words were not easy to understand. He turned off his head torch and stepped out into the black and the milk of the moon.

When he arrived home, it was dazzling daytime,

and from the time of the voice until the sound of the dogs barking a warning as he got close to the cabin, he remembered nothing. He went to the kitchen, dogs writhing around his legs, and mixed up one large saucepan and one small bowl of dog biscuits, rice, and meat. Here you go, rat, enjoy that. Here beast, you'll love that. The little dog always finished first and crept towards the mastiff's bowl to steal. The man told him sharply to not try that fucking trick. Little shit. When the mastiff had finished, the man said to the little dog, right, he's done, off you go, and the dogs swapped bowls, licking the emptiness furiously.

CHAPTER 3: THE MASTIFF

The man was still attuned to the gap of wintery time that he could not remember. He could feel the cold bone of the night on his lips. When he'd headed south to the mountains, away from the digital screens of the city, the city folk had texted him: you'll get bored there. There'll not be one of your ilk in that place. You'll be back. With that, he supposed, they'd returned to glaring at the tops of the toilet lids and their grimy data channels and hastily cut lines. The journey was short, an hour by floating shuttle, but also long—from one sphere of reason to another. As he walked off the last step of the shuttle, the grass rushed up to meet him. Water rose from the edge of the river and pooled around his feet. The mountains were flat and cinematic in the evening light, rippling like canvas. It was six miles up from the shuttle port to his mountain cabin, and he walked slowly with a fist in his chest.

A village woman was walking down in the other direction, three small black mobile phones around her neck. Two goldfinches flashed across their path. Good afternoon, they said. The man stared as they disappeared into the trees. The woman didn't seem to have heard them over her ringtones and, instead, asked whether he was the new lad living at the top. Yes, that's me, the man replied. You brought a wife and children with you, didn't you, she ventured. No, I did not, I have nothing but the bags on my back, said the man. Ah, so you'll be alone, then. No, thought the man. The phones threw out digital birdsong and data propaganda, and the woman looked at him sharply as she passed. Good afternoon, said the man. He could hear the goldfinches arguing over nesting materials. The bones of a man he loved were in the ground a thousand miles away. There were other men he had loved too, many of them still roaming the streets and living off recycled data in the city. Wasn't one of them quite close, growing spliced pig trees in a place called Parnassus? He could not quite remember. But he was intensely attuned to the moments he could not quite grasp, as if the light slipped out of his forgetfulness and weaved skeins around his body. *Day in, day out*, something was forgotten, and tendrils of light drew newness on his battered frame. And all at the same time, that feeling of who was getting in and who was getting out. He'd seen it in the woman's eyes as she'd come down the mountain with her three little phones. *I've been waiting for a guy to come and take me by the hand*, sung a chorus of voices, hurled across the years, far away from any ilk or kith or kin. The clouds sunk into the mountain's skirts and he pushed forward up the old way with a fist in his chest.[2]

After, he called a local farmer to ask about a dog he'd seen in a fat squirm of pups online. I want the one that looks like a tiger. The tiger pup; yes, he's still free, that'll be one hundred gelt in cash. The man looked out of the window of his cabin, saw how the mountains were no longer flat but growing and glooming. I'll come and get him tomorrow, he replied, said ciao and hung up. He spent the afternoon slicing great turfs out of the side of the mountain, finding dark, rich soil crawling with worms. This was the beginning of carving a garden out of the mountain. At first, the beds were fussy and tiny, just big enough for a few potato plants, spinach, cabbage, and onions. He planted marigolds about the place to attract the bugs. The vegetables that could still be bought in shops were bright but under-lit, as if the shopkeepers were trying to hide the monstrosity of their undersides— barcodes, data adverts, or disease. Like the fish, the vegetables were not really real, they just appeared in the shops from one day to the next, and nobody asked. They sliced them and cooked them the same, but some folk became ill and even noticed bleeding around their ears or mouth. The man's beds became bigger and more productive, as he shaped the mountain by hand

and tool. The trees chatted as he worked, passing messages from root to root, and the man got to work on the offerings they made to him.

The next day, he roped up his old jalopy and jumped on, trotting down the mountain at a brisk pace. As he neared the place, he noticed a heavy blur in the middle of the road ahead, and the farmer at the roadside standing. Two seconds later, he saw it was the tiger pup, fat as butter and still as death, huge eyes looking up at the jalopy as it ground to a halt. He handed over his one hundred gelt, picked up the pup, who, at five weeks old, was already as big as a seal, and heaved him onto the jalopy. Off we go, dog, said the man. The tiger pup looked sad and tired. It'll be right, we go. In a year or so, when the pup had become the guard mastiff, stretching like a shadow against the wind, they'd be long-standing members of the same working pack. But not yet. He stopped off at the town on his way back up the mountain. The dog who walked the main street grinned and showed his teeth. Fuckers, it chattered, fuckers, fuckers. The horses whispered their misery at the gates, ears flat against their heads. The voices sang to comfort him, deep in the fabric of time. Have you heard the arc has fallen? It was the same woman he'd passed yesterday. The man nodded. You'll never get a wife now, she laughed, nothing's getting in and out. God is good, and it's getting safer for the likes of me and mine, she warned. He picked up two packets of peanuts and a tin of something. Something made it through, he said.

He whistled as the skull of the mountain fell down around him. Nearly there now, tiger. The pup looked up at him, rolls of blubber over the seat. As they reached the peaks, the marten chattered from her hidden place by the pine tree. Welcome to your new job, dog, said the man. He cradled the lunk of fat on his knees, watching the mountain spires reach into the cloud in the distance. Busy day, son. But here we are.

CHAPTER 4: HARE BONE

Up by the limestone cave, the tools and colours for painting were neatly arranged. He'd cleaned and polished the thin hare bone. The ochre pooled in a wooden bowl. The shaman—a man dressed in the skins of a woman—sang his shaping words quietly on the rocky outcrop. Ancestors lined the mountain pasture among the white stones and yew sculptures. My friend, I am ready, said the shaman finally. The man looked up from his hare bone tool and smiled. He took the shaman's hand and entered the karst system, skimming the fingers of his other hand across his lips.

I was born underground, in a cavern with stalactites and stalagmites which we called statues or columns. My mother felt the pangs when she had been out hunting roe deer, and as she gasped in shock the deer scattered, barking in alarm. She walked slowly back to the cave, nodded to the spirits at the entrance, and brushed her hand along the wall as she found her way to a safe place. There were many ways in which my birth was unlikely. Yet here I was, dressed in the same woman-skins my mother bore me in. I would slip between the statues and columns, remembering little but feeling great spasms of connection with the earth above, around, and below me. The first time I made love with my man, he was unfocused and distracted, calling me by the name of another. It was the moment he was caught up in, and me desperate for warmth and recognition. You are all ego, he would say, the name is not the moment, yet he would disappear for days into the high mountains in search of the name. My legs and arms were wrenched with desire. I was sick, sometimes. After a while, he didn't come back, and I left that pasture for one across the valley, where I built little effigies out of wood and muttered into the wind. One day, he came back to me, crying like a beech marten kit, saying he would return to me and yes, he would stay. But later he vanished into the wild crooked cherry trees. Put your hand over mine, clasp it tight against the cave wall, said the shaman. The man did as he asked, and with his other hand lifted the hare bone, which he had filled with red ochre, and spat in rhythm until they could lift their joined hands away from the wall and see the blurred image left behind. I was born here, said the shaman. This mark is for us, to show where we belong and how the blood and bone of the earth will take us back. The man nodded, thinking it was time to feed the dogs and the chickens and who would weed the beds when he was high up in the mountain pastures. But he was content to belong.

Once back at the cabin, the man called to the little dog, here rat. The mastiff was lying flat out in the field but cocked his head when he heard the man's voice. Come dog, get them rats, he whispered to the little dog. The little mongrel ran towards the barn, waiting at the top of the rise for the man and his little pot of crushed and dried eggshells. Get them rats, whispered the man again. The little dog shot forward, and as the man turned the corner and opened the barn door, the little dog shot forward again, sending the barn rats flying up walls and into holes. The chickens chattered. The man scooped the bowl of eggshells into the tub of feed, filling it with grain, and poured it into the chicken's feed bowl, an old cracked plastic plant pot. The chickens pecked at the shells and the grain, the biggest white hen using her wings and beak to push the other two smaller girls out of the way. The little dog raced from one hole to another. Get them rats. The man filled a bag with kindling and bigger bits of wood foraged from the land last year. Come dog, he said. The little dog ignored him, high on the chase. Come, he shouted. The dog worried for the rats, but slowly came by, looking behind him every few seconds. Night girls, sleep tight, he said to the chickens, don't let the rats bite. Go find your brother, he told the dog. As they turned the corner to the cabin, the mastiff had his head on the gate, saw the man and wagged his tail. Come on my son, let's get some dinner. Dinner time!

And both dogs ran up the steps to the cabin, the little dog turning in circles and barking *food*. At the top of the steps, the mastiff stopped and asked for his haunches to be scratched. The man dutifully scratched the dog's rump and long, strong back legs and the mastiff stretched in ecstasy, so far that his big back feet slipped off the step and he tumbled forward. Let's eat then, said the man.

There were people who spoke of progress—by which they seemed to simultaneously—or by definition—mean 'doing, or being, good,' and people who had ways of advising you how you could do better—*you want to do it like this*, as the slogan went. People slipped into their data like ice melting in a drink. Consciousness burbled behind this elastic band, ready to be catapulted. How far away that all seemed now, as the sea of mist poured over the cleft where the standing stone had fallen. Yet there was no distance, because the data, like a tick, burrowed into him and fattened itself. On the streets of the city, where he desperately sought more data and better uppers, every digit he had pressed and every voice he had downloaded had become his singular, treasured truths. You don't need to protect yourself. You should say yes. You haven't seen what you think you've seen. You don't need to worry about that. He downloaded so many voices his phone flashed a warning. He and the people he was with were lucid with their good data, keen, tailored. The boundaries of his body were invisible, and anything could get in. He waited for the day when he could unleash the data's grip, but he couldn't go back, only forward, so he did nothing about it. Get more data. Look ahead. It wasn't long before all of them were left recycling the data that remained, their bodies more amorphous and blob-like with each passing week. Data was data, even bad data. Part of the pull was seeking it out and scrolling endlessly.

He reached his toes into the water which was strewn with a carpet of white flowers, and the first swift of the early spring skimmed past. Dogs, o dogs, what are we going to do, where are we going now? There was no looking forward. The mastiff's head shot up from the heather. The little dog cocked his head. The man breathed in the mountain air and paused.

CHAPTER 5: WOLF-NIGHT

The tendrils of mist reached down to the tops of the trees. The trees, in their way, felt the change in the air, and their voices blazed and exchanged in the fungal nodes underground. Why-so-warm. Snow-lack. Wolf-night. Wolf-night. The wolf felt the trees thrum under the earth and did not move. She could see the lights of the cabins threading across the mountains, and the deep warning barks of the mastiffs as they caught her scent. She could feel the snuffle and push of a group of wild pigs further down the mountain. She slipped into movement, and the mist lowered once more. Wolf-night. She passed the holly, clipped smart by the horses, the yew, stunted by the wind, and the mountain oak, leafless. She smelt the water trickle through the limestone; joined, if only for a second, her great ancestor wolf who had also padded this way. The pigs were too noisy to hear her, snouts down in the turf, ripping and searching. Her two sisters melted into shadow a few feet away, and an aunt and a cousin nearby. The trees babbled through the network, and all five wolves felt the arboreal voices along their spines. She spoke silently to her pack mates. We are not the wolves who come in dreams. We are not the metaphors used by man. Slowly and deliberately, the six or seven wolves crept forward.

The next day, the man woke under his blankets with the trees calling him, a swathe of chestnuts outside his window curving in pleasure in the gentle breeze. He peeked out from under the blankets. Morning rat. The little dog went through his morning ear-flapping, dog-yoga routine and trotted off yawning. The man's finger-bones tingled. Is the sky about to fall on my head? he asked the trees. A rat scattered across the rafters over his head. A chickadee, curious, balanced on the thin outstretched branch of the chestnut, whose catkins waved in the morning air. The cabin creaked and settled. He was wearing the same clothes he had been wearing for the last two years: some tracksuit bottoms pulled over a pair of old running trousers, a t-shirt that was grimy around the neck, a grey hoodie, a tracksuit top, and two pairs of socks. The little dog trotted back in. Come the fuck on, said the dog. Alright, alright, said the man. He ran through his list of jobs for the day: take dogs out, clean and feed chickens, cut down the final tree before the spring sets in, end of list. He heard a distant whirring noise and hauled himself out of bed, pushing his feet into his boots and pulling on a coat. The mastiff's head was drawn to the sky, his throat opened, and he released a torrent of deep barks. The orb semi-retracted into its plinths and its skin became discoloured. A helicopter, yellow and white, took position over a nearby peak and hovered. The mastiff roared his anger and rushed to the gate, pushing his huge feet against the lock and chain. Under the half-closed orb, the man closed his eyes. Now both dogs were barking frantically, and his head was bombarded with sudden action. It's garlen lads, he said. It'll be OK. He walked down the steps, dogs alive about his boots, trees thrumming a few feet below, and unlocked the gate. Both dogs charged into the field, the mastiff flying at the hedge and pushing his head through the thick tower of hawthorn and ivy. The little dog ran in circles and jumped, barking high and fast. It's garlen, the man muttered. The helicopter hovered a few seconds more, turned, and jerked off across the mountain and away. Right, you two, get down the bottom of that field and perform your ablutions.

Later, running the gauntlet of the road that led past the other cabins, the man and his two dogs began to hike up the skull of the mountain. The bear had visited in the night and left her berry-spotted spore at the seat where the old women sat in summer. The bear loved wild cherries and ant nests. The old women hardly returned to the mountain anymore, but if they did ever come to the place they were born, they shouted abuse—*Ewe!*

22

Whore-daughter! Man-lover! Magpie! whilst sewing. The man sighed in relief as he passed the final cabin and moved into the wild. He had fashioned one long double lead from two pieces of rope, and as he untied the little dog the mastiff stretched out on a longer range. The ghost cats of the village, white and scrawny, lined this cut of the old way, watching the dogs warily. A huge, fresh wolf scat lay in the middle of the rutted track, tapered at the end and thick with wiry wild pig hair. Both dogs sniffed it and, one by one, peed on it. Good lads, said the man. He heard an old jalopy gallop round the corner behind him and stepped to the side. What's this, rat? The little dog ran to him, waiting for his treat. The mastiff sat until the jalopy thundered past, and then woofed mightily at it, straining at the end of his lead. The old farmer and his wife looked straight ahead as they did every time, but the wife raised her hand timidly. The old farmer grabbed her hand and held it down as the man struggled with the mastiff. Steady mate, you'll have my arm off. Good dogs, sit, sit. They both sat and received their little sacrament. Then, in the distance, the heavy whirring of the helicopter. The wolf and her five or six sisters watched from their place in the trees.

Run, sisters, but not in the open, she said silently. A chorus of ancestor howls and yips followed them down the scree and up into the high oak wood. The sisters stood still as the helicopter passed overhead. We are not the wolves who come in dreams. We are not the metaphors used by man, they chanted without sound. We are not the song of the king-makers. We are not the forbidden prey of the hunters. We are not shadows. Several hundred feet below, the man entered the hidden mouth of an old way that he'd never walked before, criss-crossed with fallen trees and lined with scattered stones. The jalopy. The helicopter. Wolf-night was coming, but he did not know when.

CHAPTER 6: BODY

You could think of it as a pause between letting your breath out and drawing your breath in. Within that space is a separate universe where thinking becomes diminutive, a little rag-tag bunch of characters with lives of their own. Narratives shoot back and forth like tree roots communicating between the fungi. Salute them. Greet them. But do not be taken in by them. *But what is getting out and what is getting in?* Whatever is getting in or out, thank-you for your presence—but not now. *And the people who progress, and tell us we want to do things like this?* They are most welcome to pass by, unattended. The man closed his eyes as the others on the screen in their little data houses did the same. I will accompany you on this journey today, continued the voice. I am here to guide you in the universe between breaths, and to bring you back from those narratives that hurry across your landscape. Be still. My pronouns are they, her, and we.

The man felt the prickling sensation of each toe, first his little toe, whose curve he knew as feeling, then his middle three toes, warm in their centres and cooler and fizzy on their edges, and then his big toe, thick like a tongue, lined against the round edge of his slipper. Harmless. His feet slowly changed form and grew roots down into the earth. Tubers birthed from the top of his foot and leaves broke through into the molecules of air. He felt the hollow spaces inside his legs come alive with blood and sap and bone, each moving against the other and expanding outwards. The left leg first, then the right. He hovered around his shinbones as they floated up and down. The sensation in his thighs, his crotch, a warmness, and safety, that travelled to his belly. He softened his belly, which rose and fell, holding fruits seed and animal flesh and pulses inside. But what is getting out and what is getting in? He felt his body swerve and rush in space as he followed the thought, seeing the jalopy and the helicopter and the wolf and the trees all pouring up out of his fly button and into the cabin. They crowded up around his forehead like flies and crawled down around his ears and mouth. If you have slipped into virtual reality, said the voice, gently come back to your body. Here, in this little universe between breaths. A broiling roll of anger rose inside him, a glance, a look up and down, a word of criticism, a hundred times or a thousand the sense that his body, his mind, his full self, lay in the mire and would never get up. His eyes itched to open. He settled down into himself, feeling the hairs on the back of his neck, the sensations on his face. He focused on the expanse of birdsong above the retracted orb. His breath was shallow, the tiny universe a distant blot on the landscape.

The little dog waited at the barn door. The man pushed his stick into the mud as he idled past. Come on rat, let's go. The little dog ran ahead and scouted for ghost cats. One cat, the ogre the mountain folk called Stain, waitedby the bins. Stain met the little dog with an arched back, spitting. Leave Stain alone, rat. The little dog skirted the hissing cat and ran on ahead, stopping and looking back every few minutes. In the distance, he could see two of the mountain folk coming towards him, the ones he called the Saints: her, big shades and a pink mac; him, a walking stick and a scowl. The little dog ran to them and jumped up around their ankles. The man pushed at the little dog with his stick. As they passed, the woman smiled thinly and greeted him. Her partner, who no longer spoke to the man for reasons unknown, pulled his jacket up around his chin, head down. Sorry, said the man. God with you, said the woman. He turned a few minutes later as the two erupted into conversation, and saw the machinery on their backs, sleek and cold in the evening light. He's a bad wolf, they said. Dirty. Come on rat, said the man. A shard of glass lay in the middle of the road, glinting like a jewel. Little dog sniffed it, licked it, peed on it. A bit of their sainthood fell off, the man told the dog. Leave it. Up ahead, the road shimmered and warped into rays of light. Many insects rose before the falling of the light. Some of the light collected at the edges of the village, channelled into the spaces between tree shadows. Often slices of light rested on the limits of the village and the martens and bears came to rub against them, feeling the hairs on their backs and their haunches rise into the heat. The man owned a field where the light spooled and quivered, but only in the morning. The field was called *light-only-in-the-morning* by the people and animals who knew. He many times found traces where the wild pigs had rolled in ecstasy in his field in the early hours. A crow and a magpie brawled amongst the last light. Will we go back to the cabin, rat? The dog trotted ahead then. Stain stood at the bins, ready to fight. Over the roof of the ruined cabin, he saw his own, its orb beginning to curve up and inwards. The skull of the mountain was hard and cold as the light died. The mastiff was already barking within the outlying limits of the cabin. The man wrapped the chain around the gate and closed the lock. We're in for the night, lads. Watch out for intruders, beast, he said to the mastiff. Across the way, the couple with their data protection and inserts plugged themselves in and he heard the metal shutters slowly lower around the sides of their cabin. It's a weekend kind of place, said the mountain folk, the city has things that we need. The man shivered.

If you were caught up in an outside narrative, come

back to your body. Even if you are convinced it is the end of the world, stay in the moment. Inside your head, allow the little physical moments that have collected there to drop to the lower part of your skull, free up the front of your face and lift it up to the light. Nothing is happening.

CHAPTER 7: WAR

The man left a napkin of bread and cheese for his friend where the water started, a jumble of rocks with a pure, thin stream of mountain liquid out of the karst. The dogs strayed out into the mountain pasture, which stretched out to become an amphitheatre of limestone and holly, grass cropped short by deer and the cows and horses who pastured there in the summer. The war was finished now, but then came the reprisals. All the mountain folk crowed, the war is over, the war is over, and the man's friend believed it too, because he was tired of so many calamities and privations, of dying of hunger. But the winners had a desire to kill. Queers and gypsies and reds and witches, brothers and sisters, the evil eye. They killed his friend's parents and his sister for a crime they were never able to prove, that they'd fed his friend's lover who was hiding in the mountains. All were dead now. Only his friend remained, pining for his lover, and starving again in the high pastures with the sunlight falling around. Come by dogs, said the man. He felt eyes on his back. We'll go home the long way.[3]

The mastiff first, then the little dog, then the man,

walked by the mare's water at over four thousand feet. The mastiff stopped to drink, wading in to his belly and taking great slurping gulps from the brackish tarn, the little dog with delicate little sips from the edge. Just ahead, the ground dipped into a gully where the wolves had laid down a kill or two. The dogs sniffed around a pile of bones. The man looked closer. They were not human. A cow's skull, the thighbone of an adult horse, still with gristle on. Wolf saliva was poison to the livestock, and a few calves and foals, despite surviving an overnight attack, died hours later from toxic shock. The hunters unclipped their guns from their belts, said they were out for wild pig, and the next day a headless wolf was found hanged by its back claws from a roadside sign. The leaders—the king-makers—nominally penalised the hunters from time to time, but hunting was their right after all. Meanwhile they scoured the mountains for people hiding after the war. A great circle had been drawn in chalk at the entrance to the village where once-hidden warriors were dragged, shot, and left to rot. The bear sniffed at the limit of the circle, seeking carrion. Sometimes the man found human bones high up in the mountain, strewn across the high plateau in weird patterns as if thrown for scrying. The mastiff loped on. The little dog, incandescent with joy, raced up out of the gully and flew across the ensuing stretch of grass, ears back in the wind, circling round and round smiling.

That looks fun, rat, said the man. He put out his arms and whirled around in circles, again and again until he landed hard on the ground, the dogs rushing up to nose and lick him. He laughed. Tiny alpine daffodils peeped out of the short, wiry grass, spreading across the high field in a carpet. Where was his friend now? Perhaps he had found the cave with columns and statues. Maybe he sat slumped beneath the fiery blurred hand painting, weeping. I see you, my brother, whispered the man. Enjoy your bread and cheese—bread from the bread jalopy, floury and soft; cheese with a thick waxy rind from the endless plains on the other side of the mountains. In the spooky night, it will nourish you.

In the city, the war was forgotten. All enemies of the state were locked away in prisons and mental health facilities. There were other things to worry about, such as building new places to live and bulldozing the old. Workers walked the scalding streets with bleeding hands and dirty faces. Some died in the heat and were lifted away by drones and buried in unmarked graves, families unknown or, more likely, unregistered in data streams. Data was everywhere, plastered across the sides of scaffolding, travelling across screens in cafes, and pinned onto trees spliced with peacocks. The word *freedom* was on everyone's lips and t-shirts. People talked about the war in the past tense and avoided family members who had fallen foul of the authorities.

They visited new supermarkets whose shelves were mostly full, the ruins still smoking around them. The floating shuttles that hummed in and out of the city took people to new natural rewilded enclosures and pig grids bright with new names and brought them back within the day. Some people changed their own names, or their children's, or doctors stole babies from imprisoned women and changed their babies' names. As people sought data in the streets, their heeled shoes clicked against the tarmac, or along the perfect rows of flowers that spelled out the city's new name and the year. A young boy sat bundled up in a doorway of a decaying row of single-storey houses with dirty, fly-postered, graffitied walls, his little dog cowering at his feet, and a bowl and a message laid out in front of them. *Out of data. Please help.* His eyes rolled in the back of his head. Helicopters criss-crossed the sky above him menacingly. A drone hovered nearby, filming. *Take a floating shuttle for a day-trip to the pig tree plantations*, read a sign above the boy's head, *safety assured!* These undesirables, said someone as they passed. How disenchanting, said another. Nobody stopped. This is how the world ends, giggled a group of friends, blazed on data, clicking their heels with delight. As they posed for the drone, the light rested on their faces and melted slowly into their skin.

The man's friend gasped in pain as he dragged himself out of the open and into the oak trees. The ground thrummed beneath him. We made it quite far, he joked ruefully to himself. His lover's arms—his forearms, precisely—were the image that had become plastered to his memory, as if no other parts of his body had ever existed. Now, not even his forearms. Such light, fine blonde hairs on freckled skin, the veins of his arms always slightly visible, the skin tanned from working in the sun. One less shepherd in his vest. One less steward of the land. The man's friend ached and bled alone on the forest floor, dreaming of being alive and his lover by his side again, watching the sheep with the bitch mastiff baying at the perimeter.

CHAPTER 8: THE ILF

Along the old way, primroses, crocuses, forget-me-nots, irises, dead-head nettles. Dock leaves, daisies, and dandelions. Reborn honeysuckle and bramble. A roe deer barked ahead as the man and his two dogs trod the earthy path between tumbledown walls. The mastiff strained on his lead. On his left and right, there were slipways up and over the walls where the little dog would stop and sniff and sometimes follow on. The chestnut, oak, ash, elder, hawthorn and birch that formed a canopy over the track were alive with chickadees, goldfinches, woodpeckers, pigeons, jays, magpies, crows, bullfinches, yellowhammers, dunnocks, and robins. Higher up, buzzards and vultures soared and circled. The old way was in fact a multitude of crisscrossing wild highways, flight paths and underground networks. Badger, marten, fox, wild pig, roe deer and wildcat. Bear, red squirrel, wolf, red deer, field mouse and lizard. The thrill of multiplicity teased the edges of the man's body. Tiny field mice holes dotted the sides of the path, and marten scat. Goose grass caught on his top and burrs and ticks at the end of the dogs' coats. Bees hovered around, dipping into open flower heads. The shaman had walked this path, many thousands of years ago. Love to thee, brother, murmured the man. The man's friend, only eighty years before, had fought his way through the summer bracken away from the guards. Male lovers of men, female lovers of women; or simply women born as ovals, and ovals as men; or with a tone of voice disliked by the king-makers; magicians gulping and overflowing with difference inside them; the first shapeshifters, neither fully animal nor completely human; or solely humans, with the power of the green goddess at birth. There was a terrible burden on his people now, and everybody worried about what was getting in and what was getting out, and moving forward, and teaching folk *they wanted to do it like this*. He knew that being away from the smoking city and even the village with the fallen arc of rock, and stewarding the land, was no solution. Sometimes he used to say to people, when the planet is too toxic elsewhere, at least you'll be safe here. But now nobody could get through the rubble and scree, could they?

There was little truth in between the words that were spoken. The nugget of earth. A cowbell chiming in the distance. But everybody wanted to face truth these days. At the lip of the village, beyond the chalk circle, some of the mountain folk had constructed a barrier of gorse and brush to keep the diseases out. Still, though, they lunged their jalopies up and down the mountain daily to buy fruit and vegetables studded with battery codes, and after dragged the barrier back into its place. In the valley, green fields were slowly being transformed into great grids of spliced pig trees and their cloned pork. The king-makers poured money into the public coffers and created an *Interdisciplinary Land Fund*, which they used to wine and dine dignitaries and show the dignitaries the wild places where the money would be spent on rewilding the space into pig grids. The man spent quite a lot of time thinking up shitshow versions of the acronym: the *Inappropriate Licking Forum*; the *Imp Liked Fornicating*; or *Idiots Lose Fings*. The king-makers told the dignitaries that in this post-war landscape the most important thing was growth, and by growth they meant radiant success for a top tier ethno-state, which is what had been happening anyway and the war propelled. Winning a war is always a radiant success for top tier folk. But still the farmers and other mountain folk painted their jalopies the colour of the *ILF*—a rosaceous purple bordering on a bruise. The *ILF* had various functions and sub-groups, including the *ILF Family Network*, which promised to unite mothers, fathers and children in the viewing spaces that bordered the pig tree grids, in order to teach them about something they called Nature, how it related to ethnicity, and to get them to fill in forms that measured levels of enjoyment. It was found that the *ILFFN* was best suited to neurotypical children who had one masculine parent and one feminine parent, to honour the post-war sentiment of sensible regrowth and suitable demographic regulation. In fact, the woman with the three phones from the village down from the cabins was the statutory leader and de-facto recruiter for the *ILFFN*, and often trotted her jalopy from village to village, even cabin to cabin, praising the well-dressed children that she saw with their young cool dads and chilled mums, and turning her dark eye to those other different humans who floated on the periphery, speaking into one or more of her phones. One day, when the little dog had burrowed his way under the blankets for the fifth time and for the fifth time thrown all cushions to the floor, and the man shouted *for fuck's sake rat* and laughed, he heard a great rumbling in the chest of the mastiff and suddenly both dogs rushed to the gate, heaving at the chain and lock. The woman with her three phones called at him from a distance: is all well? do you have a moment of time? It is and I do, shouted the man, and as he walked to the gates the dogs lessened their racket. Good boys, he said, good guard dogs. What can I do you for? She said that she was making a survey of the cabins and needed to know today how he used the land and who would be living here in the future. The man replied that any official questions could be dealt with at the council pod in the village. The mastiff growled.

Good lad. The woman said: but it's for the *ILF*. Well, next time I'm down, I'll pop in and talk to the council person, he said. He thought, *I Like Finish*. No companion yet then? No companion yet. She eyed him up and down. Your sweet peas need water, she said. Thanks for your time, he offered. I've got some oregano, would you like some? I'll take a bit. Nothing gets in or out these days. Safe, though. I dry it and put it in jars, like my mother and grandmother before me. Do you know how to do that? Although it's hardly a man's job.

CHAPTER 9: HEADS IN A LANDSCAPE

In the villa of the deaf man the walls went from pale to black with faces and limbs: the witches' sabbath; Saturn devouring his son; men reading; half-submerged dog; fight with cudgels. The mountain rears against the high lands of the crumbling wall like the shoulder of a giant. Black stains slide down the precipice from high peak to valley. The sky is a sickly yellow away into the distance, beyond the shuddering peak, and the mist rolls over the slicks of black oil that run like paint into the lines of water falling. Mountain oaks line the base of the peak. The trees twitch in dynamic forms, bleeding into the mountain as the high wood enters its skirts. White streaks scratch the gloomy matorral in the foreground, strange orifices in the wall that should have been investigated years ago. Five faces glare out from the high mountain plateau, crystallised as dark amber, one more hidden than the rest.[4] This is the man, cocooned on the corner of history, divine and murky of forehead. One of his dogs, half-submerged, peeks his head out from behind the sandbank of the sun on a facing mural. The painter awaits the end of the world. The man's friends are caught amidst the strands of conversation—five cows on the other side of the peak—bones and tissue, she caught it—who is that yonder—we are not their metaphors—the wind, the wind forever—wake up! And I told him, I said there would be a wine waiting for him at noon, after the donkeys were safe and high up, but he was sure to be mistaken, to be angry, to not understand. There is no way he could like me, not a man this side of the mountain. They can't see me, can they? I'm out of shot. The sage cried out to me that all would be well, this life was built by my ancestors and would continue beyond the crumbling borders of the mural. Keep your eyes down, lad, they look for something in us that they cannot see.

It repeats itself. I carry a big wound in my peculiar flesh. My own, real image was carved from the villa of the deaf man and hammered to boards for exhibition. I painted the poem for a no, the myth of syphilis, and now the heads in the painting. This is possibly my finest work, an obscure, dusky flesh lining the walls of a house that no longer exists. Now I speak to you across time and space to clarify my position. I had a first-hand life of pain, terror, and hysteria. Also, comfort, contentment. Nobody asked me to paint the heads in a landscape, they spoke through me and will speak through others. There are those who questioned the casual and direct way I channelled their voices, but this is merely a usage of pockets of time that are consistently found in the general skein, and I have no fear of death, or certainly not in the sense you might. You may fear, like me, the way your body fails and the way the limits of it are simultaneously hard edges and blurred lines. This body will end. But beyond such momentary narratives, I tell you it is possible to outwit the linear. What is linear is already dead. The way you are born, the way you enter a narrative *not* of your choosing, and the way you walk out of it, are all ethereal promos, even if they seem profoundly vital. *Coming up into the mountains, everything is so clear.* You'll see the way I painted the sky—all moody bruises and elsewhere-eggshell blonde—well, that is also the colour of an infinite network of affinity you may choose to be part of. That is to say, if you look carefully into the black oil, you can see crevasses and within these depressions, tiny caves. The figures contained therein are hard to make out but, one day, you may be surprised to suddenly see their faces gawping at you from the front of the canvas. Behind the walls, when the murals were hacked off and exhibited, many folk only saw the walls of the house, red and naked, but there were others who saw unbounded landscapes of anxiety and joy. I am not alone in this. Linear perspectives are truly the most dangerous human instinct. Once I was deprived of my own image, and the data it generated, I was able to travel between many years in an extremely short time, and in this way spooled long shadows that in their own time joined with the shadows of others and created innumerable connections hitherto unimagined. Such is the way of putting brush to canvas.

During the time of snow, the man had felt a new feeling of desperation which in turn created a renewed strength in his body and mind. He had been sitting with the two dogs at his feet, feet up on the sofa, big log on the fire—an open grate in those days, before the tube burner. Flames shot up the chimney, high, too high and with a sudden unexpected might the fire began to roar. Sparks began to fall in great sheets from the chimney, and the roaring sound travelled up the old flue. The man ran to the front of the cabin and watched with horror as the chimney spat sparks and flames into the freezing sky. The dogs milled. He ran down the steps, opened the gate and with the dogs ran towards the other cabins, shouting aid, aid, please aid, and he saw light behind the metal shutters and shadows shifting and lowered voices and data clicks. The mastiff had run ten metres down the way, and barked a high, nervous yelp. The little dog cocked his head—what now? Fucking hell lads. The man ran to the barn and grabbed the ladder, charging back to the house and tripping over the dogs who were confused at this late-night panic. The chimney bellowed, its voice impossibly loud in the icy air. He slipped through the ice until the ladder was propped against the side of the cabin. He filled the mop bucket at the tap and climbed the ladder, lying flat on the blocks of ice that lined his roof. Reaching the chimney, he poured the water into the fire, listening to the hissing as the chimney fire died down. The heads in the landscape nodded grimly, but proud. The man breathed. Well, that's that, then.

PART 2

CHAPTER 10:
TRANSHUMANCE

The little bull and the placid herd are dots in the colossal landscape. Closer, the ring through his nose is visible, and the chain round his neck. A stunted oak hunches a few metres from his thick shoulder amongst the vastness of grasses, gorse, heather, fern, and bramble. Plumes and sheets of mist roll across the highest plateaux, a place of many names: prao–hafod–shieling–alp–booley–yeilak–bald. This is also a place of nomadic beings. The trees move slowly up and down the mountain, speaking in years. Fire runs across the gorse from time to time, scattering birds, and snakes who practice their frantic infinite *s* away from the scorching. There is movement everywhere always. In the time of snow, the man and his dogs can go anywhere and seek out the tracks of the mountain hare. Only four or five mares remain this high up, scratching through the ice and snow to the meagre grasses underneath. The first jalopies arrive in early spring with mares and cows kicking and stumbling inside. Some mountain folk still trudge up behind a horse or two from the bottom of the valley, shouting take, take, go up, go up. The old ways are well-trodden, and have been for much more than a thousand years. Soon, the man and his dogs must look for the paths only they use, empty except for them even in spring and summer: bands of mastiffs prowl the mountain near the herds, a ferocious white bitch wearing a collar studded with spikes educating her two massive pups; the herds cling to the jalopy ways and public routes, and the cows lower their horns and dash at the man and his dogs if they pass between them and their calves; the farmers stutter and thunder up and down to the shieling to stand in groups and discuss the herds, fix fences, always with binoculars around their necks; helicopters lurk in the skies, some heaving great bellies of water; the floating shuttle spews out small groups of visitors who jalopy their way to the tops, taking photos and shitting in bushes. The mountain is littered with tiny white mounds of brown-stained toilet paper. Foals, unsteady on their feet, soon learn to race at their mothers' hind legs. The stallions turn their backsides to anyone passing, except the farmers who coo to them with calm voices and feed them hard bread. The little bull stands impassively in the middle of any path, bowing his head to the man and their dogs as they pass.

The man fought his way out of the overgrown cañada, dogs up ahead and suddenly silent. On turning a corner, he saw both dogs with their tails high and tense, sniffing noses with a sheepdog with blue speckled eyes. The new dog's hackles were high, and the elevated greeting soon turned to snarling and dust. Get back you two, and he grabbed the mastiff, who settled pretty quickly. The little dog kept up the scrap, and a farmer laconically appeared, saying let them fight, I like a good dog fight. The man ignored him. Here little rat, he said, and grabbed the little dog by the harness and attached him to the lead. Now be quiet. The little dog squirmed and barked savagely. The farmer raised his stick, and the sheepdog cowered. Back off, the farmer growled. Calm. Good day to you, young man, greeted the farmer. Good day, replied the man. My grandfather used to clean this old way in his day, but nobody does anymore, I don't have time, too much to do, even though I'm retired, and you'll never guess how much my pension is. It's a beautiful old path, answered the man. It's good to keep using them, me and the wild beasts and my dogs. The farmer shouted two thousand gelt a month, the biggest pension on the mountain. Back when I worked at the central dairy, those were the days, a hundred head of cattle and that was just my father. Did you bring your cows up the mountain yet? asked the man. Too early, lad, and anyway I'll sell them all next year, there's no money in it and the mountain's ruined, half-empty even in summer. I'll go to the city in the winter, I bought a new flat there, you know the new postwar builds? Everything new, nothing to worry about for ten years minimum. I'll come in the summer, and we'll have a few barbecues, grow a potato or a pepper, the country is for weekends—for my daughter and her husband, and the grandkids. The city has things we all need. Ah, we do OK, answered the man. You get cold in winter, you'll be nearly dying of the cold, the farmer retorted. My grandfather and my father didn't work their fingers to the bone so I would freeze on the mountain. No, lad, the best life is to shuttle your way between comforts and follow the sun. It's true, now the stone has fallen nobody gets out or in, or hardly anybody, you see my new jalopy—and he pointed to his sleek steed waiting roadside—I roll over the rubble like a tank, but that's me. Paid for that in paper gelt. The man was at a loss for words. They say a disease is coming to the mountain, you'll know you've got it if your fingers tingle or sting. Come dog—the farmer hit out at the sheepdog with his stick and was gone.

The tiger mastiff was a nomad to the gum of his bones. In his sleep, his mastiff ancestors told him gruff tales of the peaks, wolf-night after wolf-night when the witch and her sisters circled the round stone cabins into which the shepherds pushed the lambs at twilight. Then, they were six or seven dogs each wearing a leather clasp around their necks studded with nails pointing outwards. It was called "bringing points." Every generation there was one dog less, but this was before the machines and jalopies appeared. For miles in summer, the mastiffs would follow the herd across the flat tops, down gullies and through sparkling woods, up dusty drovers' paths lined with limestone which opened out into terrific expanses of green. Then each would take up position, some stretched flat in patches of shade, others on lookout. A mastiff can sense a thing from a mile off, hear a thing when there is no sound and see a thing when the view is bosky. Be gentle, his ancestors would tell him, but fierce—so he was. When awake, he would stare down at the man and the little dog from a hanging rock, completely impassive and alert, or lie flat out on the cold plastic the man used to cover the beds in winter and fall back to sleep. In the autumn, his ancestors would then tell him, we would wind our way down with the flocks, proud if not one animal had gone to the wolves. One of those wolf-nights in high summer, we remember it—how could we forget?—the wolves had come at them in force, and one of our team, a great white bitch mastiff, rose on her hind legs and grappled with a snarling wolf. Soon, blood and flesh were flying and the shepherds shouted and held up wands of fire. The bitch mastiff snarled into the night, leapt out o' the circle of lights, and there was an illustrious sound of the stars rushing to meet the earth and she was no more, gone to the wolves. Another time before, that same white bitch mastiff disappeared into the mountain and when her time came whelped eight pups with wolf in their eyes and muzzle. The shepherds took them and drowned them that same day. The tiger mastiff woke and stretched, jumped on four legs and barked. The man called down to him in the field, hey dog, that is a prolific sound, what goes there? But *there* was only a trio of ghost cats balancing along a fallen wall half a league away. The mastiff settled back down to his trance. The wolf was running in and out of his dreams. The shepherds came to us in skins and left bones for us. Soon we would join them, spidery tails curled around their ochre works of art. The tiger mastiff rose up in a furious torrent of noise, suddenly, as a ghost cat made its careful way across the roof of the broken-down cabin nearby. That dog's bored, shouted a neighbour. The shaman sang his painting songs high in the limestone caves and called for the man and his dogs to make tracks up the skull of the mountain.

Now the city shimmered between bomb-blast and luxury tenement, and the wandering ways were largely forgotten. Each year, the man tried to open back up the old country paths, and each year the weekend folk blocked them back up with the refuse and detritus from their summers—neon-pink prawn shells, half-wrapped parcels of baby shit, cloned faux-charcoal, great clumps of unwanted plant life doused in toxins, empty bottles of alcohol. The mountain, this wild place of nomads, became—for a gloriously hot and sunny time—a canvas for human activity which, in the rubble of the city, could be easily hidden and fenced in. Each year, the man dug trenches around his garden and down into the valley to carry the soaps and petrol and oils and urine and shit that the summer folk excreted and poured from their windows.

CHAPTER 11: CAMOMILE

Count one. Count two. Then six or seven vultures join the spiralling above the orb—a coil of birds high in the white sky, gleaning leftovers from wolf-night. There was a click, and the kettle stopped boiling. The man opened the fridge door and the light was off. He leaned over, long forearms gleaming in the evening half-light, and tried the switch to the bedside lamp that he used in the kitchen. No light boys, he said. His mug sat empty with a few dried camomile flowers scattered at the bottom. It was said that if you were caught picking camomile the guard would take the money you had on you, scan your data, and make life difficult in ways unspoken. The camomile grew in blankets high in the mountains as well as in stripes along the old ways and pitted roads. There were places the guard could never find you, just ask the man's friend. The mare's water. The cave of the mouthful. Never-green woods. The burnt house. The give-me-something grotto. There wasn't really much to do when the lights went, just wait. The man imagined somebody fried like a cooked chicken on the light grids. Probably a blackout. But yes, somebody was always frying out there somewhere. There was a process of belittlement in the air, in the light, in the dark, and, in the dark, tiny steadfast shreds of emotion that recognised the belittling. The process was ancient and human, like sleight-of-hand. Beyond the process, which was turning folk blind and heavily sedating them, were the instinctive lines of communication across generations and species. Instead of drawing in and hiding behind glaucous eyes, due to felt-unfair criticism or taught phobia, *à la* the process—these instinctive connections were profoundly non-pedagogic—non-linear—non-polarised—and rooted in a flowering towards affinity. The man was protective of his camomile, and grateful for it. The camomile, grateful for the picking—just as it was grateful for the grazing—grew back in even more dramatically ornate length, width, and breadth each year. The shaman in his women's skins picked it to crush with fennel, plantain, and nettle for healing, and as an offering, when he would burn the sun-shaped flowers and inhale the smoke. The man's friend picked it where the guard could not find him, boiled water over a cave fire and left it to steep, just a few flowers or the infusion would be bitter and undrinkable. The mastiff and the little dog would lie in it and roll, or trample it under their feet as they roughhoused, making the man swoon as the sweet smell hit him. Camomile, when applied to the eyes, stymies the creeping ague of the

55

process. Suddenly, the kettle clicked back on, and the fridge began to hum. Soon, the man was pouring boiling water on to the flowers and smelling the sweet-bitter aroma of his tea.

The man had pinpointed three spots on the mountain where in summer he could forage wild oregano. Some years previously, across the mountains and down into the lush valleys further south, a woman had walked with him up a granite slope to a rocky outcrop and showed him the long stalks of oregano with fat green leaves on either side, a dying flower speckled with white crowning the tower. Pick it at the base, she said, but don't pull out the roots. Always leave some. Even so, they had walked back laughing with armfuls of savoury herbs and shredded and chopped fresh leaves into salad. The woman was wise and lived free in her jalopy, cantering, or walking on a long rein, from one landscape to the next, always foraging wild things and making gifts. For the man, she had woven a dreamcatcher from hemp and found beads and nut-casings to thread through it. Now, the man went from place to place for wild oregano and left some growing. Picking oregano, said one of the mountain folk as they passed him in his labour. I am, answered the man. My spot's further up, replied the neighbour pointedly, hopefully I won't lose it to someone else. But you're fine there, and they walked on. The man breathed and muttered under his breath in a language the neighbour would not understand: *Idiots Lose Fings*. The walk back to the cabin, without the dogs, was quiet and peaceful. A couple of ghost cats flitted across his path. The blackbirds called and tumbled through the gorse. Not a jalopy or helicopter to be seen. The edges of the chalk circle were washed out with recent rain, and the barrier erected by the mountain folk was shedding foliage onto the old ways. A horse or cow had pushed at it and nibbled at it and now it was stricken and half-bare. The little dog cried and jumped in circles at the gate. The mastiff waited, impassive, until the gate was open, and then he lumbered down to nuzzle at the man. Home now, said the man. He dug some strands of string out of a box and tied up bunches of oregano in the kitchen. He saved a few short, wispy stalks for dinner. He crushed five slivers of garlic from last year's cloves with salt in the pestle and mortar, scraped it into an old jar and poured in some oil and vinegar, and added a big dollop of mustard. Not much left. But they still had mustard in the shop down the village—that was still getting through. He put the lid on the jar and shook. He ripped some spinach leaves into a bowl, chopped the oregano and mixed it with the leaves, and poured over the dressing. Pretty fucking delicious, if I may say so myself, he told the dogs. They waited for something more substantial—a bone, say, or a sausage.

The sun had been shining for two days, maybe

three. The potatoes were starting to show, planted with the waning moon. Time slipped from the man's grasp like water. He welcomed it, spiralling with the vultures in a loop. Many people spoke of the end of the world as if it would come tomorrow, but there was time yet. Great gloopy oil slicks of it, oozing between the stunted holly and high mountain oak, sliding down the scree and karst hollows, pooling in centuries and minutes at his feet.

CHAPTER 12:
APOCALYPSE

The fungi and other minions of the green god shared the news through touch and moisture. A drumbeat pulsed through them. Little filaments vibrated their timpani, wet nursing the roots of trees, talking to them about nearby water, warning them of imminent attack, stealing and sharing and introducing. The mycelial knew what was going in and what was going out—they were the interconnected highway of thought and deed. The news was, in the whole, transmitted, and across great distances. The tree herds stamped and snorted. The elder wove their spell, shooting forth flowery white constellations only to transform them into black jewels. The curved hollows, gaping mouthfuls, and raised fists of the karst system were gateways to vast reserves of water. The tree herds and flocks of grasses and brush siphoned these secret underground plunge pools and stood, glistening, as the bear and marten sipped droplet and teardrop. By the time the news reached the green god, the network was a symphony of bellows and sharp bow-scrapes. The green goddess lowered their antlers and roared with anger: *Harm is in us*.

Instead of worrying about the end of the world, you might want to think about what's closer to home. Castles in the air, pipedreams, or delusions hardly help on a day-to-day basis. What's more, drifting into white-out or semi-conscious understanding of what is *real*—which is post-war regrowth in a state of hyper-vigilant independence, a collective grasp of ethnic identity, and the controlled relationship between human technology and hybrid nutrition—is both dangerous and illegal. We are talking safety, abundant use of state-generated resources, and border control—not technological libertarianism or multiethnic global oversharing. There was a round of subdued approval and polite applause as the leader of the *ILFFN* gathered her chirping mobile phones in one hand and clenched her jaw. Welcome to the proud seat of the *ILFFN*, mums, dads, and kids! It is so wonderful to see so many normal, natural families interested in learning more about protecting ourselves from fake governors in freefall, and about the farming methods that allow us to withdraw from the network—our freedom, that we are implementing. Families have to be safe and eat safely! Here at the *ILFFN* we will show you simple and progressive ways to support these methods—and how to become part of it! Thank-you. There was more muted applause. We now have time for a round of questions from you, the consumers, and members of our little big family, so please speak into the drone mike if your turn comes. The drone hovered near a lady with a worried brow: how can our kids get the benefits of Nature, and stay safe? she asked politely. Great question, and lovely to see you here—I know your mum and went to school with your dad—as you know all normal kids need to be at school or plugged in at home learning knowledge directories for exams. The great news is they can do that here too, amongst the spliced pig trees, in the centre of nature's revolution! The *ILFFN* is building a bespoke tech hub by the visitor's centre, keeping stock of the fallen arc—right now, as you know, it is not easy to get in or out, but safety is safety. While the arc site is secured, kids can use their own home tech hubs to search for information about Nature, live data experiences, open virtual natural worlds across time—I mean, wow! Everything here—every tree, every field—needs a new name, and suggestions are welcome. To sum up, we're saving ourselves by keeping our natural borders safe, and that's what we need to pass on to our kids. The woman's brow uncreased slightly and the drone moved on. A man, dressed smartly in brand-new, high-end hunter's gear, said: good evening and god with you. God with you, too, the leader of the *ILFFN* replied. I wanted to ask, now that we need to be so careful about who gets in and who gets out, will there be a renewed control of influxes and outgoings? Wonderful! exclaimed the leader. Of course, as you know—and I know you know, I've known you since you were knee-high to a grasshopper—there is a strict influence from above on who we can let in and let out. But *ILFFN* members will be the ones who pass on tips and advice from the viewing platforms of the spliced pig tree plantations. Here, our mantra is: "You want to do it like *this*"—it's about showing folk how to do things properly, with scientific and academic backing. On top of this—yes, there's more—any naysayers will be reprocessed and sent to the Friendly Stateless camps in Parnassus. So—nothing to worry about. This land is our truth—and the sooner those who are not of our land get their jalopies and drive—the better!

The leader of the *ILFFN* slid into her jalopy. She was a woman of this land as her parents and grandparents before her. There were many whom she considered interlopers, outsiders. Different folk. It was a relief to be leaving the past behind, to forget about the war and consider a new kind of fairness. Forgetting, but officially—a pact of forgetting.[5] As she trotted forward, engine purring, she made a mental list of actions that would really start to put this place on the map: seal the deal on that land up yonder, where the horses had started to gnaw and worry at the gates, and extend the spliced pig tree grids; blast the rubble into the valley entrance, secure the pass, and pacify any anti-border *ILF* members when the arc was fully impenetrable to outsiders. Install the new names for the county and its villages—names that really defined who they were and how they were related to the king-makers. Pass legislation to keep the wolf under control, and kill the ones that sniffed around pig trees or new installations—a fenced reserve, where the animals would run free inside—and competitions to hunt those proud beasts in the name of the ethno-state. Safety. Her mind was working so fast. All the love I have for this land and building it anew. She loved her place of birth, felt it in her bones. She slid up to her cabin and slowed the jalopy to a halt. The cabin was a sleek impression of tradition, rebuilt from the ramshackle hut her great-grandfather had built, but using all the most modern and refined materials. She pressed a button and the faux-wood door lit up. She pressed another button and the cabin itself was illuminated, bright and immaculate. Her garden was stuffed with brand new reproduction items from yesteryear—a fibreglass cow, a shining bronze plough, and a faux wicker beehive—all equipped with alarms. Never before has tradition been so grandly displayed, she said to herself. I am the envy of the old folk and of those who cannot afford to upgrade like I have. Pork and chips for tea, methinks, she smiled, and went to her fridge stuffed full of grace-and-favour pork products, and clean, barcoded potatoes from the good supermarket with the fecund-looking fruit and vegetable section. Never-mind what they looked like underneath. Glory be. Health and safety are the symbols of the future.

Not far away from the *ILF* leader's synthetic mountain home, the wolf heard an incoming hunter before the hunter heard her. Of course she did, but that did not settle the fur on her back. His machinery of harm was designed to destroy her. This is not harmless, thrummed the roots and mossy voices under her paws. A robin landed on a branch and opened its beak. Grim, grim, grim, it chanted. The wolf paused at the thick body of the walnut and whispered to her sisters, when the buzzard flies low out of the trees, all is not lost. The hunter was half asleep in reverie, gun resting on his knees, sandwich wrapper on the floor by his feet. *Suddenly, the window opened of its own accord, and I was terrified to see that some white wolves were sitting on a big walnut tree in front of the window. There were six or seven of them. The wolves were quite white, and had big tails and had their ears pricked like dogs when they pay attention to something. In great terror, evidently of being eaten up by the wolves, I screamed, and woke up.*[6] Oh shit, thought the hunter, that'll scare the vermin off. He looked around to see if anyone might have heard his wail, skewed by his loony daydream. Monsters in my room at night, he shuddered. A buzzard flew suddenly

64

out from the canopy of trees, shrieking a warning. The hunter felt an electric current of pins and needles in his toes and fingers. There was something hot-unfamiliar-under his skin.

CHAPTER 13: FALE

The ruins of the cabins sprouted cow parsley and nettles a metre high. Fale hitched his globe boots to his waist and adjusted his vac mask. The sky was pink and purple hazy. In one hundred years a riddle of weeds and ivy had choked the mountain hamlet, gulping through cracks in the roads and softening the topography. Goose grass masked the signs and took on the forms of fruit trees and water troughs. Fale felt like a wizard, or a bird, so high and alone in the poison wild. A trio of roe deer plunged past the nearest cabin, whose cracked and broken orb glinted dully in the rosy light. Fale knelt down, the silver foil of his globe boots bunching up around his waist and picked through the detritus of a life left long ago. A wooden mortar, flecked with moss and shell. A long length of rope, tied in the middle, and frayed now at both ends. Pieces of clay pots rimed with soil. Rotted garden plastic spiky with grasses. He touched the plastic through his vac gloves and it disintegrated, the fibres melting into the atmosphere. The skull of some big animal, clean and long-staring, still with some of its teeth in the front cavities, balanced on the ground, skull to the heavens as if it had been placed there. Looks like a dog, thought Fale. A big one, this mountain mastiff. Any beasts had been left to fend for themselves after the process-end, and not many had known how to survive, or had been shut up in barns and slowly died of thirst. He'd heard of mastiffs gone to the wolves, integrated like, or ripped to pieces. He'd heard of mastiffs who'd remained in the mountains with the last of the herds, many animals dying of the slash-burn after process-end. People had died of slash-burn too, of course, in their millions, and that's what everyone wrote about and built monuments to, lines of post-enders in globe suits ugly crying behind their vac masks. The edges of the last cities were venomous and uninhabited. Even before the process-end, this place had been a wild outpost, the odd loco living off-grid and cowering from the belittlement measures of the harsh years prior to the tempest. The ethno-staters exploded rock formations and hemmed themselves in with geography and guns. Fale was itchy under his suit and mask and his skin felt hot. The things we won't do for love, he remembered, thinking: won't freeze my heart in a hold-all until the right man or virtual man comes along. His work here in the mountains, cataloguing and remembering, filled him with purpose that ate up time. He was heavy with the apocalyptic gloop of the world, even though really everyone seemed fine in their globe suits and looking up to space and waiting. Is it time yet? *It is, it is is, it is*, as the song went.

We were as thick as thieves. When we'd got through the acid showers and were allowed to take off our vac masks, you'd kissed me with a slow tongue. I've never ripped off my globe boots so fast. How I would love to regale you with tales of rolling in the hay and planting wildflowers in urban parks, but those were only dreams I had and wished I'd never woken up, where the wolves ran free. The sky always pink and the tarmac thick with blue weeds. We went to the museum together and looked up names on the monuments that made us laugh and cry. You told me how your grandmother had lost a lover in the process-end, the father of your father, and how even your grandmother had lived with burnt skin and took hours at the hospital having implants and grafts. We both had many lovers. This was normal, of course. You lent me books with words like ethics and promiscuity and care and freedom in them and took videocalls from lovers who were faraway and lovers who were nearby. You called me friend. I took photos of you with your top off so you could share them with your lovers, because you said you might never look this good again. You had not a single burn on your body. You told me how you'd change your name to that of an ancient god who worshipped cock, and I believed you. I still do. You showed me how I could be a king or a wizard if only I would just believe it. All I had to do was sit in a chair and call it a throne, or pick up five objects and sprinkle them with salt, and then they would be magical. I told you I loved you. You made me a list of songs that explained why love was something out of your control and not in your near future. *Even if it means hurting us both, the wrongs become rights when we stop and wonder how, look at us we're better friends now* by somebody Greek or Italian was one. *You can come inside me* was another, the disc had butterflies on the cover.[7] I listened to the thunder in the acid clouds and lowered my gaze.

Fale bagged up the items—except the dog skull, which he left balanced on the ground where, he felt, it had been left as an offering. That was impossible, but well. His lover, long gone, had told him to leave offerings wherever he went. If Fale was to keep one beautiful thing from that whirligig time, then that could be it. He spoke into his academic grab-phone: I'll be at the old shuttle port in an hour, send the intern to pick me up. His supervisor said roger. He set off through the rubble of cabins, and spotted vultures circling overhead. The mountains stretched before him into the distance, gloomy and bruised under the pink hazy. Really, he thought, this mountain has not changed for a thousand years, and will not change for a thousand more. Forever, all my life, I will bury my good love in the toxic soil of the highest peaks and wait to see how nothing stands the test of time.

CHAPTER 14: THE LITTLE DOG

The little dog cowered at the feet of his master in the rubble of the city. The city was streaked with hallucinogenic rainbows, or so it seemed to the dog's master, who was off his face, telling the dog many stories of the unicorns and dragons that sailed high above him and screamed. The little dog's forehead was immer creased in worry. He was small, brown, with white socks, a white spot on his back and a tiny wart on his left hind. His constant thought was *food*.

At human shin height, the tarnie dog travelled through the streets. He was close to drains and rats and discarded food and shit, all of which filled his every waking thought with greed and necessity. He wolfed down half a brown disc of gristle, ingesting some of its wrapping in the process. The kid who had hoofed it in his path said, cute dog. The little dog stopped and shimmied up to the kid, tail wagging. Have a fry, said the kid, and he threw it so the dog would leap up and catch it mid-air, which he did with a snap of his jaws. The kid fussed over him for a while and when no more food was forthcoming, the little dog trotted on. In the rubble, someone had thrown an unclosed rubbish bag, and the dog growled at the cats gathered around it. They spat but ran. Some little yellow pellets and brown slime were made short work of. Wrappers and paper lined with food grime also. A sweating construction worker, already half dead from the heat, hands bleeding, shouted oi fuck off dog, this is private property, and the dog understood. He ran on. A busy street, trousers and naked legs and leggings and tights and billowing dresses. A human shit, curled into a drain. The little dog sniffed it and wolfed it down, bobbing his head forwards and backwards to force it down his throat. He continued, licking his lips. He stopped outside a place that smelled of yeast and warmth and food. The woman working behind the counter said look, that dog again, and she threw him some scraps. The dog wagged his tail and growled as the people milled about him, then grabbed the last of the scraps and ran. A bird bone lay before him, and he ran with that too. The sounds of jalopies and humans and sirens and construction and wailing and music came at the little dog from all directions. He ran to his master who was sat bundled up in a doorway of a decaying row of single-storey houses all with the same dirty, fly-postered, graffitied look. You came back, dog, said his master, smiling. Here, come in, and he lifted the blanket so that the dog could curl up in a nook of his body. Safe now my little love, and can you hear the boys singing in harmony and the drums and strings, like we are in a show and everybody is watching. Is everybody watching? Suddenly, his master looked scared. The dog curled up closer. Soon, a boy came and said, hey mate, let's score. Got any gelt? The dog's master fished in his pocket, unwittingly poking the dog and waking him up. I've got a bit, what you got? A bit too. Let's see. Shit yes, my friend, we've got enough. The dog's master left his blanket and bags in the doorway and they walked half ran round the corner, little dog following. Give us a half a synth, said the boys. You got gelt? Yep, here, and they showed the gelt. Here you go. The boys skinned it and injected it, sauntered back to the doorway, and sprawled. The dog lay by them as they began to gibber and rave, eyes pixelated, the city forgotten; and the city passed by them, blind and sedated. Later, one of the boys frothed at the mouth and claimed himself king maker. The other sensed military personnel in the ruinous heart of the other, beat him, took his bags, and ran. The dog shrunk into a corner as his master stretched out on his back, unconscious. A deep blackhole opened without sound.

The little dog nosed at his master, but his master was blue. He barked, high and sharp, *wake up*, *food*. That guy looks dead, man, said a passing citizen. The drone'll get him if he is, answered his mate. The dog looked up as a machine floated down from on high, and he heard a human voice, scanned subject dead on arrival of drone, calling bag team. Quickly a team of robots had the dog's master in a body bag despite the dog's growls and worried whimpers. Team dispatching body to disposal centre. The dog's master was not there, and the little dog sat and waited. He waited for twenty-four hours, receiving the occasional titbit or kick, and then moved on, his forehead creased and his belly empty. Some years passed as the dog crept from bin to bin, human to human, hideout to hideout. He got thin and snappy. One day he was locked up in the back of a jalopy and taken to a cage that smelled of elsewhere, surrounded by other dogs in cages yelling let us out, let us out, all day and all night. The little dog charmed the volunteers at the refuge, and the day the man came to meet him, a tiger mastiff puppy cowering behind him in fear at the cacophony of dog anxiety, they said to him, this little dog is the joy of the orchard. The little dog ran up to the man and ran away again, jumping in a circle on all fours and lying on his back as the volunteers rubbed his belly, good dog, fine dog. He ignored the mastiff pup, who was afraid of him. One day they would be mountain brothers, circling the peaks—free dogs—but not yet. If you could give us fifty gelt to cover the costs, it'd be good, said the chief volunteer to the man. Now that the war is over, people are just buying puppies and dumping them as dogs saying they cannot afford to feed them, or that they worry about disease, or, maybe, like this little guy, they just wander the streets. Hello, street dog, said the man. Will you come with us? Yes, said the little dog. Come then, said the man, and he bundled the lanky mastiff and the little dog into the jalopy, wound their way from Parnassus, past the pig tree grids and trotted up the mountain to the top. Welcome to your new job, rat, said the man quietly, as the orb began its night-time journey, and the little dog was transfixed by the skull of the mountain.

CHAPTER 15: FORM

At first, the man believed magic was in small and beautiful forms: witch-stars, Mondrian rectangles and squares, pentangles or the ouroboros—the way something was shaped was surely the power of it. But after a short spell the mystique of contour and outline was lost on the man, as the weeds choked the pepper plants in their arrow shapes, or the myriad fiddly triangular fences that needed to be chicken—and wild pig—and bird—and ghost cat-proof overwhelmed him. What good were three potato plants enclosed in a pagan star? How could he pickle and preserve cucumbers and line up the labelled jars if there were merely a few plants thirsty for land beyond art history? After a few years bewitching himself with this aesthetic conundrum and offering tiny shells and seeds at the magic spring under the weeping willow, he said: fuck this.

He spent many mornings felling the chestnuts that sprawled over the top of the field, dropping their catkins and leaves and other contributions, and reseeding and growing endless thin shoots a metre or two high. He lined up the wood in different sizes, some for kindling, some for fencing, some for burning. Something in him had shifted. When he had first stepped off the shuttle, life was a dream. The fantasy of data had burrowed deep inside him until his own voice was no longer his own. Everything he knew had been taught to him in a place so far from the land that the edges of his body had disappeared. He was a cryptograph, a symbol of fact and taught energy, an encryption that was based near his head but floated through virtual geography. His real world was tiny, a zero-sum environment. Naturally form was his religion—he himself was formless. But now he saw that the trees and their wider network of flora and fauna, who spoke under, above and around him, had very little care for structures that pleased the naked human eye. Singular shapes that appeared in the landscape were synthetic visitors and would only ever be swallowed up. The man saw that his simulated presence was alien. He ripped up the witch-stars and squares and rectangles he had only seen in frames and perceived the steep lines of the land. He thought that perhaps everything he had done was not a failure. Marigolds were established now, little colonies here and there; the places he had stuffed mown grass and weed mulch had flattened out, or suggested themselves as terraces; here and there a path made itself known; and the trees he had respectfully taken out let in light that before had been lacking. He could see a garden. With his heavy mallet he heaved posts into the ground, opening out the space—he did not think of the shape—into three large productive beds. In the middle, he made steps down towards the middle of the field where the garden, in its current incarnation, would end, and dropped off into space. The trees, frustrated by this carving movement, sent little messages across the network, which appeared to the man as new life—sprouting leaves—on the posts after they had been in the ground a couple of weeks. The man was conscious of the trees' voices, but to him they sounded like birdsong or crickets chirping: he tried to hear the shape of them, unaware that their voices were penetrating the newly-solidifying edges of his body and wrapping their filaments around his veins. To the left of the new beds, he opened out another space, obliterating the pentangles and smelling the explosion of rich earth. The work did not require human words. He called the dogs and chickens to him and told them to work their way around the edges of the new garden. If they found a hole and could get through, it was not finished. Found one, shouted the little dog, and tried to wriggle his way through. Get back, ya shite, said the man. He wove some thin wicker into a lattice and blocked the hole. I'm in! crowed the big white hen, and called to her sisters. Get out little dinosaurs, warned the man, and shooed them out in a flurry of resentful feathers. He hammered some thicker poles across the gap and turned to the chickens, smiling. The garden was settling into itself.

At first, the man believed work was a calling with a beginning and an end. Many times he would wake up on the forest floor, dazed, and think of all the things he had to do and groan. This was a difficult condition to heal. He was baffled by the advice—sought in books, launched upon him by passing strangers and friends and, especially, the king-makers—that sucked the strength out of his body. You want to do it like this. You want to do it like this. *You want to do it like this.* Slowly, though, the garden and he cooperated through failure and doing to find that, although sometimes tips and advice were good, a lot of the time words were like emotions—immutable convictions rather than frail outcomes of repetitive trying. He distanced himself from too many words, even though they had form and would suddenly crystallise in the air in front of him pear-shaped, aquiline, mandorla, dog bone, nebula, butterfly curve or ovum. He didn't know how to call the things that the trees and plants communicated to him, mostly because he hadn't recognised it was happening, as such, but his own form gained edges and roots and sap and bark. His movement through the garden and the mysterious language this created became his work. Each time he left the safety of the orb and opened the garden gate, there was an action that he saw needed to happen, because the garden told him without words, and this exchange made him content. He saw that the words he spoke were mostly empty simulacrums or reflections— or, at best, a mangled representation of the words of others who had perfected language as a medium of diagnosis. He sat on the old, pitted stump he called *chair* and pushed rich soil gently into little plastic cups, made sure it was firm, then used a stick to make a hole in the middle, drawing circles with the upper end and keeping the bottom of the stick in place. The hole would keep its shape. He reached into little marked tubs of seeds he'd dried from last year—leeks, fennel, lettuce—and sprinkled them into the holes, before firming them over and dripping water gently into the cups, using an old vinegar bottle.

There were black tomatoes, nipped by the early morning mountain fog. There were potatoes that never appeared. There were slugs and snails and birds. Birds that got caught in netting and died horrible deaths. Seedlings that in no way took, planted too early. Mulch that was too full of ash from the fire, or compost where the rats took up residence. Moles burrowed under the fennel and great cavernous underground highways swallowed what was above ground. Mountain water knew its course, which at times was through the garden and back out of it, leaving a morass of mud and surface water. The time of snow was long, and hard, and the garden was a metre under it. The winters came mild and the voices who gave tips and advice said it was because of the war, because of disease, because humans had bled their poison into the earth and skies. The summers came hot and some people were found fried out in deserts that had been cities, or the autumns came wet and people were drowned in rivers that had been roads. The voices said the world was upside down, and that everybody should worry—that this was the beginning of the process. In this way, most every human was belittled. There were glorious moments of shocking colour and afternoons of new potatoes cooked over the fire, sprigs of mint colouring the water. Green tomatoes fried in oil, courgettes grated into salad and smothered in lemon juice, fennel and garlic roasted in the coal oven. Spinach in salad, wilted in butter, cooked into stews and bakes, eaten fresh in the garden before the next thing. Roses suddenly bloomed and then wilted. None of this was a simulation, but a cycle of work embedded in the body and populating the mountain with a series of real forms that knew no words.

CHAPTER 16: ARC

The mountain folk wanted to leave the world a better place than they found it, they said. In the post-war, when what had been bad must now be good, arguments and discussions about remembering and forgetting were commonplace. Everything that had to be forgotten became, by law, forbidden conversation. What was *better* should be framed as perfection with a very high colour. The king-makers told the people that this perfection was a complex series of secrets that they might never know, but that which would be the saving of them. At the same time, the process started. In fact, the process had been happening before the war, was codified, and boggled during it, and continued as a complex series of mirrors after. Data was a marvellous tool. That ideas were short and immediately resolvable, rather than long and sometimes arduous, lent data its' motor. Everyone was belittled. Everything was better.

The arc must be secured. The shaman, in his cave, moved his hands above the fire and jangled his necklace threaded with bone and nut casings. As I flung the arc over the pass, so I will build the rubble into a cliff and make so that the pass is blocked, he murmured. The village folk waited for the lorries and bulldozers to arrive, but for days nobody came. The farmers rolled over the limestone in their sleek jalopies, bringing gelt for their wives and synth fertiliser for their pig trees. The anti-border villagers wrote letters to the council pod or walked in, red-faced, and demanded action. The council people, now controlled by the *ILF*, said their hands were tied, but things would be better soon, they could have that in writing. There were mutterings of disease in the city, of people who bled at the eyes and hands and mouth. All were on tenterhooks about what was getting in and what was getting out. I have the right to go back and forth if I so wish, said one farmer. If you want to come to the mountains, take the shuttle, said another. The mountain pass pulsated with a forcefield that filled the mountain folk with deep worry. Visitors who walked to the pass saw nothing except a gap in the rock, which they passed through easily. The bear watched from her place by the pine tree and saw what she had always seen: a disturbing hole in the mountain that she would never venture into. The man's friend, up by the mare's water, remembered the day his lover had arrived, up from Parnassus, under the arc and into the valley. This is another world, he had said. The city folk arrived on the floating shuttle and asked for directions to the wolves. The wolves circumnavigated every mountain pass by whispering to the rock and the water in the rock until it shifted. Perhaps this was the real reason why the mountain folk were trapped in the valley. Or perhaps, as others suspected, the mountain pass simply must be secured, remoulded, renamed, and forged as a solid iron symbol of safety. The arc was for some, as it turned out, a gate. One day, the man's friend made a run for it, threw himself in a river down mountain, and, next thing, in some shrubs. He could escape but injured in the leg. A bullet passed into his knee, which might lead him to death, but slowly. He crawled to a barn near the village and wrapped his knee in his shirt which he ripped into strips.

The two men held hands in the field. Around them grazed their donkeys, placid and wide-bellied. A commotion in the barn caught their attention, and fingers slipped out of their caressing. One of the donkeys started. Steady girl, said the men. They walked purposefully towards the barn, looking around and behind them for the king-makers' guards. Take it easy loves, said the men as the donkeys flicked their ears and threw their heads up. As they entered the barn, they smelt the metal of blood and the man's friend shivering in the corner. What happens here? I got shot by the guard, I'll die soon enough, answered the man's friend. There was a look of recognition between the three men. You're the lad who had sheep up on the mountain with your man, they said.

I am that lad. Your man's good and dead, they say. He is that, and the man's friend broke down and wept. No doctor, no medicine, no guard, said the man's friend. One of the men went for warm water and a compress of plantain and calendula. The other sat by him and held his hands in his. The man's friend began to speak. I am tired of this persecution. My man is dead, my mother and sister, too, them for taking him food in the mountain. My friend has been leaving me good bread and cheese, but I made a run for it, down and out, through the mountain pass I thought, to a new place. But now I'll die and that will be everything. The donkey herder listened and held his hands. Then he spoke. You will not die. The other man returned and began to wash his wound. I need to get this bullet out, otherwise that's it. The barn door was closed. Do it, said the man's friend. It took a long, hard time but the bullet was out, and the blood flow was staunched. What now, said the two men as the man's friend groaned in a stupor of pain. In another place and another time this would not end well, said one. We would all be rounded up and shot by the guard. But here under the arc of our home we will make a family of three, and the donkeys will be well cared for. The three men were frozen in the dark light of the barn, their faces peering out from the landscape like ghouls, one soft and kind, the other hard and worried, the last in a rictus of agony. In the background, up in the elevation of sky pasture, some beasts, probably donkeys, were scattered to the high corners, with the broken arc of the mountain pass a dagger in the oily distance.

Six or seven wolves floated like mist down from the mountain and took watch outside the barn. We are not your metaphors, they whispered. We are the last of the shapeshifters, not really wolf and hardly human. You are not asleep. You are blind, sedated. Do not come close. A doctor will not help your mind to assimilate us. *Your* ears prick like dogs when they pay attention. Inside, the men heard the wolves low-pitched language and did not understand. But nobody came.

CHAPTER 17: FIGURE IN A LANDSCAPE

The man was still attuned to the gap of wintery time that he could not remember. He could feel the cold bones of the night on his lips. This forgetting could be the reason of his life and the cause of his doings, and yet when the fields were sparkling with spiderwebs in the early morning he felt only the great oubliette. Often, on the most clarion of evenings, when the sun shone through the cabin doors and the dogs twitched and hunted in dream fields, he remembered that this had happened before, somewhere else. But the gap remained. One of the most prominent searches in his data retrieval in the city had been for lost time. There was a full business related to the search for lost time that had made many people very wealthy. They said that time was made to be hunted, like a hare. The hare implored the hunter in vain—and the hunter, answering, said, but I only possess the skill of death, not the power of life.[8] They said that time was a piece of string, and any string could be reknotted and therefore made whole. They said that time was a cup which could be refilled. They said that time was an ocean, and all oceans had a floor, however deep one had to travel to get there. Dixie, said the man, and grabbed his coat.

In the centre of the wheat field, a figure sits with their head bowed, features smudged in charcoal purple.[9] The figure is vigilant about those who regard him, yet a heavy inaction weighs on his downcast brow. The wheat around him is also bowed, parting into infinite storm rumblings, and the metallic joints of trees shudder in the background in ancient post-apocalyptic futures. Which choice that the figure made is trapping him in the image? Which page that the reader turned has opened out into this boundless field? Which time is it? He is stuck in terrific torment in the canvas, immense drafts of gale pulling at the edges of his body and a black central line drawn from the top of his head to the tip of the picture frame. It is not the fact that people give him tips and advice, but the context of incipient blindness caused by the process—this can also be named as *ambition-for-mass-extinction*, *earthbound-disconnect-desensitising*, or the *evil-eye-brouhaha*. We seek out the gist in words, but little is digested-human communication is not rich in exchange. Instead, a series of monologues joined in the middle by memorised passing phrases overflow us. Everyone oscillates in a universe, but nobody knows how the universe is grounded in the body. The figure awaiting the thunderstorm is grimy with sweat and plagued by flies. The atmosphere is thick and oppressive. After years in the mountain, slipping between ancient ruses, he can't hear the voices that say to him—*give me what I need.* He can't hear the woman who arrives, high on data and, after a few days lying in the sun, says to him, face serious, man, it is so good for your head to be in the country—do you know it? Or the hippy's friend who, visiting coke-addled, tells him stories of his childhood helping his grandfather pick olives before leaving a trail of bloody discarded tissues on his way back to his jalopy. The guys who pass by to take photos of themselves in situ and process the data as sunlight, faces fixed to their glowing screens. Let me tell you about what it is to be queer, and how this little mountain holiday will do me good, before rushing back to the ruined city to plug themselves in to the sideboard. The man even thought he had no part in this, despite him being the other mostly willing node in each connection. But a critique of authority whilst using your own to dismiss others? What a shit painting. The air is so thick the man wades into it, huffing.

What to do while waiting for the storm to break? The sky has been bright white all day, and the mountains laced with pearly sheets of light. Soon the thunder will rumble in the distance. The whiteness of the sky contrasts with the creeping dark clouds, tiny, hardly visible at first. The sun beyond the pallor is so hot it must be very close above it. Every time the man moves it is to suddenly become still again. Each stretch of his muscles fills him with exhaustion. Entombed in the centre of the canvas, his solitude emanates out to all who survey him—get that man to a city, sharpish, and have him connected. The messages kept on appearing, every morning after a night on the uppers: I miss you; I need you; it's my birthday, you should congratulate me— even now, you do not write; I know you are doing your Nature thing, but what about me? The man breathed in deeply and remembered the words for what they were— narratives soaring like vultures above the mountain peaks. Isn't solitude—when observed—just another means of communication, without words, perhaps? The orb protected the man from the damaging rain that had started to fall, and that smelled like a dark room in a club. What is your metaphor? The pins and needles from the heat. The story of the guy with two dicks. The goats, bridled and saddled, used for racing in backwater towns. The skull of a baby mounted on a post at the entrance to a grand mansion. The cigarettes stolen from the child with the acid t-shirt. The microsecond of pain before the premium experience. The bloodsucker who left the goats lying bloated legs up in their field. The baby before death, chirping and swaddled. The heat before the end. The mass migration of trees into huge sinkholes. The recorded sound of birds at the fair. The fear of time. The uprising of the ictus. The failure of the seedlings. The flowers of the walking dead. Our own network of poison that exists in our bloodstream, micro-poisons that communicate with each other under our skin. The luxury of blindness. The sharing of fluids. The scratchiness of living. Dark fire on the horizon. In the story of the forgotten dark, the past's voice speaks in a language unknown but close by, and then the journey into the skull of the mountain.

PART 3

CHAPTER 18: 1010

The hailstorm hit, golf balls of ice cannoning off roofs and walls and stone and wood. Seedlings, stripped of their leaves, disappeared. Water gushed suddenly through a hitherto watertight area of ceiling. Lightning ripped the sky apart over the standing stone. The sitting place outside the cabin became a lake. The big dog roared at the sky. The road washed away. The cabin stood, firm but shaken. How long before the mountain breaks apart and the giants hurl limestones at the valley?

The man had spent a lifetime trying to answer questions with no answers. But this mountain work, was that a question with an answer? There was once a worker, a farrier by trade, who was taken into hell to toil.[10] He laughed, after a sad while, at how hell was a fine place for a farrier. "Work sets you free/ in gas chamber number 3", they would say to each other. Gallows humour. The long path to capitalise on the beautiful, patient, often burdensome work of individual humans as they looked up from the land is, indeed, the history of humankind. The farrier, whilst in hell, was tasked with a disgraceful piece of metalwork, which the devil had commissioned for the entrance to his beloved, and profoundly functional, flaming pits of despair. Of course, the farrier could not refuse. His is not a tale of singular heroism, in the way those stories are tailored by some cultures, nor an ideological think-piece, a political or cultural history of the ethics of work. *This meditation is* not *a discursive reflection on a philosophy of interdependence.*[11] It could offer up recognition for the farrier, the details of whose work in hell were memorable. The farrier used the same flame from the burning pits that contained millions of screaming souls within them. Such was the employment, the master's tools in the master's house.[12] The metal was strongly wrought, the lettering that was to arc above the gates to hell simple and stark. The farrier was steady in his work. Sometimes rain would fall in the underworld, or grey flakes that looked like snow. There were even rodents in hell, and birds that flew above the spiralling plumes of smoke that rose from the abyss. Did the farrier weave a secret message into his work? Did his work answer any questions—to which, elsewhere in life, the farrier had found answers elusive? Once he had finished, and in other pieces he created for the devil, it is true that certain subversive symbols—upside down letters, strangely-turned curves, uneven light-fittings— became apparent. The devil himself noticed some of these rebellious flourishes and passed by with his pitchfork, striking the farrier and branding him. Still, the devil needed the farrier. The skill of good and beautiful work is a precious commodity. Only in very few dreams can it become a source of personal enrichment. The devil became caught in a power struggle so nightmarish that he lost his authority to another demon just as cruel, and the farrier was able to escape from hell. His two-hundred-mile journey from the underworld has been recounted, in part:

I present to you the wren Fonsu, in the dark green woods, and across the flat, unploughed fields of a post-war world. How strange. A jalopy wrapped in plastic and bungee elastic as if it were a gift. A woman pushing two well-dressed babies in a pram. At times we switched from winter to summer in one frame to the next, but the bars were all shut, year-round. There were recently-cut paths that we had to traverse, forged in the war, returning to their original selves—bramble, holly, oak saplings—and in summer the flourish of growth made some ways almost impassable. Yet behind some rusty gates, hidden and busy people had begun to tend their land again. The green of vegetables—potatoes and onion tops at times and heaving frames of runner beans and cucumbers at others—came to us in momentary snatches. Our thoughts were preoccupied with the past. Kind Fonsu walked by my side, even so, and held my hand when I shuddered as the past rushed up and showed the teeth in its face. We spoke, then, of the shape and feel of the rusty gates, and other metalwork and such experiences of shoeing horses that we had had before we were ushered into hell. Horses are funny when you put shoes on them. Some will get so comfy they will sit on you until a sharp jab in their ribs moves them from their slumber. Others, even after the first time, will get up on their hind legs and try and fight. Some remember you and wicker softly with pleasure as you unfold your tools from the leather. Of fences and balustrades and gates, we could talk at great length. Work was never finished, but only in progress, and so we talked of upkeep and repair, failure and breakage, weather damage and damage by living things, and above all these we spoke of the illusion of longlastingness. Always, at this point in the conversation, Fonsu would lean over and kiss me on the lips, for a long time, and then wink. He loved to play, did Fonsu. My world of vision was only his face, even if his face was multitude.

The storm rumbled on. The path to our mountain home separated into infinite blood vessels. *Is that the wind from the desert song? Is that the autumn leaf falling? Or is that you walking home?* sang Fonsu. I was thinking how much a waste all this faded beauty was, given the hell we'd been through and the uncertainty of our future. Any time now, Fonsu could be taken from me, or his mind could collapse and he'd leave anyway. Or the voices that spoke to him might come back from their holidays. But we kept walking, away from whatever it had been. It was funny how from one moment to the next, I could slip from depression to quiet contentment, as round the next corner I felt quite improved, and squeezed Fonsu's hand gently. Hell, so close by, and the inexplicable hatred of others for our bodies and minds, so recent—but life was also here. Just as soon, I might fall back into the dark—it is the walking, I had a mind to say to Fonsu, that keeps us in our bodies, although we carried on in silence. That garden we passed way back, the one with the many jumbled sticks, I said. Yes? I am thinking of my own garden—the back, tall with weeds and choked fencing, the front, with flowers revealed and assembled plants—the one I had before the end. Tell me, said Fonsu. It was a warren, a maze. I love that the weeds stood as tall as the trees in some places, and in others I pared them back to let other more edible plants push through. The back and the front were really the same thing, or indistinguishable from each other. It was woozy with time. Season after season; and yet the huge labyrinth of colour and fruiting darted across moments with clearly non-linear dimensions. The reason I mention from *back to front*, Fonsu, is an idea I borrowed from a dead man. He always used to say to me, as we read books in towers, or drank dark liquor at night, that men like us come from behind. Fonsu snorted. That's what the bullies used to say, that's for sure, and then us queens as we screamed and cruised for boys. I hear you, Fonsu, I replied. Yet this beautiful dead man was tired of the bullies—and even sometimes of his beloved queens, scandalous, on the defensive, and ashamed as we have learnt to be. He was tired of any burgeoning authority, even his own. He was a man of work. His work was a great adventure of the mind, and his objective was to wilfully play with this sense of our belittled essence, our primal being, as being understood *in retro*, by whose authority, which he called *behindsight*.[13] His ideas always held something beyond my grasp, which I loved—all ideas, after all, are unfinished and, as one wise woman said, *deep at play in the makeshift*.[14] What is a world where we have been perceived and catalogued after the event? Diagnosed *a tergo*—from behind? What if diagnosis—or its opposite, madness—rested on a framework of opposites that, for queer folk, was not a recognisable structure? Was this idea itself—the diagnostic nature of language as penetrative, phallic— something that could be broken down? Of course, in the dramatic world of ideas, any potential dismantling of Western logic is called *apocalyptic*—and the aftermath certainly made the magpies screech outside the window. Yet it is merely a different shape. We make this brain teaser physical all the time—fronts and backs are sites of play, of penetration and opening, of tightening and dilating, of refusing and failing, of liquid and mess. There is no opposite, but multiplicity. One night, over a bottle of wild cherry liquor, I told him all these beautiful ideas were implementing their own problematic diagnosis within the fabric of the idea itself. Exactly, he cried. But where does that leave us? Still no potatoes for dinner. Thus, I came to the work of *behindsight* in the timeless, time-laden garden.

CHAPTER 19:
BEHINDSIGHT

The journey continued in the good old days (when times were bad). Hell felt many moons away. But of course, it was always there. The moons moved in circles. Suddenly it was summer and the garden was yellow and cracked. The cucumbers and peas lay like straw in their beds. The sticks foraged to help them grow were tied back together in groups leaning against the fence that separated the garden from the field. The chickpeas had been left to dry but still showed some parts fresh. Ripe, they were little soft green buttons. Sweet, delicious. The dill and fennel had begun their yellow flowering into seed, quite beautiful. The broccoli had only ever produced a few florets, and if watched carefully, tiny weevils and bugs could be seen teeming at the base of the flowers. The aubergines flowered purple and then grew unlikely black globes, which the plant, although small, supported on its own. Their creamy white flesh was rich and sticky when cooked. Rainbow chard grew everywhere; red, white, and yellow stalks in profusion and many leaves.

Good in salad. Wilted as spinach. Plentiful and good. The sunflowers had started to turn brown—not quite as bold as last year, heads small and lacking in seeds. Where potatoes had grown in great clumps, the soil had been turned and beetroot planted. The first one was the sweetest, roasted in fennel seeds with its wilted leaves on the side, pink flesh and purple juice staining fingers and chopping board. These were the riches at the end of summer. The moons moved in circles.

It was autumn. The garden was scattered in leaves which the man raked up and spread over the empty beds. Then it was winter, and the beds were a metre under snow. A rainbow hung over the valley in spring. A fogbow, too, in whose centre the man could see a tiny shadow of himself. There was a time when the garden had returned to mountain. An old woman with a glass eye and a metal hip, who sometimes passed through the village, said (every time the man saw her, which was every day for two months in summer) I see you have taken over my mother's land—she grew mountain spelt, cabbage and potato. Then it was left for twenty years to gather bramble and nettle until the man carved the garden back out of the mountainside. Before the woman's mother's toil, it had been mountain once again, garden before. The land slipped from mountain to orchard from generation to generation, but each human generation thought theirs was the centre-point of the land's fame. If the story of work has any words, it would be these. You heard the night filled with flies and the bats swooping down from the stars; paradise, for those that felt it. Such relaxation, such warmth in the night-scented stock. It was summer again.

It may take time to explore the value of these repetitive cycles. It may not. Firstly, the value of garden work was not just to produce goods for others to enjoy, which, it is supposed, is a definition of work. Secondly, to understand the philosophy of work is to treat gardening seriously. Laughter is not desirable. But what becomes of this crescendo of ideas? Gardening, after all, is little like that. The crescendo of growth in summer, for example, is a game we play with the non-human which we eventually lose. There is no end to this game except laughter. I recall from before the downfall, a sort of work pamphlet appeared, way back, wrestling ideas back from conclusive high drama:

With the permission of the Minister of Societal Collapse, the Institute for the Harmonious Exchange with the Non-Human is being opened in T-----. The Institute accepts adults and children of all gender expression. Study will take place morning and evening. The subjects of study are: gardening of all kinds (rhythmical, medicinal, and others). Exercises for the development of kindness, work, attention, hearing, forgetting, emotion, instinct, and so on.[15]

Understanding the value of garden work might take into account, but not too seriously, failure—the failure to understand. A thing is not just what you know of it. Quite the opposite. Even the medicinal garden was a place where time circled very dramatically, and the man was dipping into work thousands of years old—and, more importantly, not looking forward, but beside a web, or net, of work, to exchange lost or forgotten failures. He kicked off some serious dancing in the rhythmical garden. But failure—this heady sense of not quite succeeding, and trying again—was the best dance of all. The neighbours, whose handiwork the man imitated somewhat successfully over the years, thrust their glowing eyes through the hedgerow and said, simply: you want to do it like *this*. Even then, he learnt. Head down, counting seeds, he mostly ignored them. What crystallised in his mind as he gardened was the sense that any work could be approached with playful apprehension. There was no believing, just a gentle well-read attention to other people's weak or strong narratives. On the other hand, the man knew of many beautiful gardens making good lives. He could not shut up about them but often struggled to marshal his thoughts beyond the romantic notion of the garden itself. Fonsu snorted. *Actions, not words*, he said. But the man was trying hard to reach a successful conclusion. If he couldn't analyse this, what was he good for? Data was so riddled with conspiracy these days that, ideas became religions quite quickly. A counter-argument, robust with answers, was surely necessary. The strong idea of ancient and primitive work as, conversely, the logical outcome of failed modernity, loomed large. A series of ethno-states have appeared that, currently, only allow entry through fallen arcs, lingering tunnels, or lazy bowers. They are sustainable. The garden, on the other hand, as I have mentioned, does not grow into an either/or dichotomy—and this, my friend... but Fonsu, behind him, stopped him by putting his arm on his and when he glanced back Fonsu's face looked serious, concerned. Hang on a minute—you've got something on your face. Where? There, Fonsu said, and poked him in the eye, guffawing. Let us stick with the details, he said. Neither rich nor important. Nameless, often. Outliers, but people of interest. Not born creatures of the city, also perceived as creatures, unfit for purpose. Now, in hindsight—what will we have grown, and what could we have eaten?

CHAPTER 20: GATES

Behind the high mountain gate of long grasses and sweet alpine heather exist epic, classic, or long forgotten dreams happening underground. Indeed, just a few centimetres under the heather, a series of tunnels supported by earth arches lead to a maze of rooms, store-rooms, and meeting caves the size of stadia. Below these karst caves dripping with water and pearly with age, deeper caves hundreds of metres high plunge downwards. Within these giant spaces, a race of beings—name unknown, non-human—has begun to construct elegant and huge dwellings that crowd the space in plant-like arcs and webbing. The arcs are new. At the base of the karst cave, a small aperture leads the shaman—for it seems to be him moving through the passages of the subterranean world—into the dwelling place. His hands trace the rock and along lines of language, pictograms, runes, or hieroglyphs. The wall is a story, ancient legend a hundred metres high. The smell of roasting meat wafts up from the cooking places and disappears through the elasticated holes in the limestone. In alcoves, in dry corners, red plant-like vegetation, and some blue, hang in bunches. Then, tendrils or fingers appear around a corner in the stone maze, and feel their way across the shaman's face. This is really happening.

First, the shaman wandered beneath the great story wall—if that was indeed what it was. He ventured to understand what these creatures did, and why. He watched as the tendrils moved their way across the face of the limestone, feeling into or over the weird shapes and hollows and tumorous growths of the epic. He could not ask, but over time he began noticing patterns. There were many collectives of tendrils, which seemed to act together, but in separate groups across this part of the cavernous underground amphitheatre. Sometimes a group would feel together into a hollow in the stone, trace tendrils—about five or six different single fronds, like fingers—for a time, and then move to feel over a lump, brushing against it back and forth. What was this—remembering? It seemed not a dissimilar activity to the symbols and signs the shaman would paint higher up in the karst system. But the shaman felt these so deeply, he could not understand how these tree-handed beasts could feel the same. But maybe. After many hours of observation, the shaman had come to realise that the same tendrils were doing the same thing over, and over, again. Very slowly, very deliberately. Later, he moved down through the branching walkways of the dwelling place towards the smell of roasting meat. On turning a corner, he shook from the tip of his feathered head to the hock of his skin-covered feet. A pile of folk from up beyond the mountain gate lay at various angles, naked, to one side of a great furnace, which was being fed medium-sized trunks of ash by a group of tendrils. He started back, suddenly feeling exposed and endangered, like a single roe deer at night on the peaks, but the tendrils waved the same calm shapes at him as the others, the stone-strokers. Will you eat me? Their gestures suggested to him that they would not. Nonetheless, it was horrific to watch the naked folk, still painted with woad and stained with the mud of foraging and hunting as he was, being expertly dismembered and fed onto shelves at the top of the furnace, and see—and smell—the fat drip down into the fire. By the green god, and the horse goddess, and all the animal deities—the tendrils had looked so harmless. These voices would never be heard again, would never be given their own hieroglyph, or understood. After a while, he could make out another group of tendrils portioning out the cooked meat into receptacles and passing them out through a hole in the limestone to another group and away. To feed the community? To be used for scrying? Both? He backed away through the passages and watched the smoke of the furnace wind its way up towards the karst caves nearer the surface.

Round another angular corner, other groups of

tendrils caressed small blue and red herb-like plants, moving them into deeper soil or plucking them out of the earth entirely and passing them on elsewhere. Soon he was to reach an enormous opening where millions of tendrils presided over great piles of cooked flesh and mounds of coloured herbs, and a beautiful noise like music—an orchestra of a thousand nose-flutes, perhaps, or a mega-tribe of graa-tak—sounded from pillar to pillar, and it was impossible not to feel somehow aroused, even overwhelmed. He moved to the noises and smells, emulating the curving, and undulating, of the many tendrils. He had no idea what was happening. Was he in danger? Were they celebrating? Was this murder? Madness? Merriment? If he was to observe, then he should stay. If he was to raise the alarm, or save himself, he might perhaps leave. Such was the way of it. It was known to the shaman that within the great circle of time, he could never see anything new. Eye-popping, though. He wound his way up through the rooms filled with tendrils, searching for a word or definition that might describe these repetitive group tasks. He could not ask. What is a thing that is done many times, by many creatures, when that thing is the same? Was it similar to his daily forays out into the mountain to hunt? Surely this was not the same, as a hunt was always different. One day it could be a hare—a bolt out of the heather. Another day it could be a pair of partridges that flew low and speedy. Yet a different day could be, with the man, a roe deer buck, heavy over their shoulders. Was it as the herbs he tended himself, wild oregano pushed into the outsides of the cave, and wild thyme the same? The cherries he foraged in early summer, then the little yellow plums, and later still the blackberries? Journey after journey he had made to the same trees and bosky zones of the mountain slopes, year after year. Was this it? What was the work that made and destroyed things, and how was it hidden? Where was the work that did not destroy? Where was the work that could not be destroyed? Slowly, he walked up the limestone slopes of Hell and, with a click, let himself out of the gate.

CHAPTER 21: FOLLOW

Fale read the note on his grab-phone, entitled *Manifesto*:

> I have begun to follow a primitive lifestyle. I
> am anti-systems. I have quick reflexes. I hold
> advanced political degrees: Extinction Admin.
> Systemic Destruction. Impact Anti-greenwash.
> You know it is not my fault to be the first. I am
> the primary caregiver and world destroyer.
> This is joyful.

Fale was never sure about such scripts. His life was based, as per post-process-end, on action, not words. Scrubbing out through the acid showers and winding his way in his globe-suit through the wastelands, he stewarded and researched the poisoned land. He felt apprehension about glorifying anything, past, present, or future, or any time zits in between or off to the left. He cleared old ways, restoring scrubland and its borders, ripping off the goose grass from old wells and troughs and piling it in sticky clumps, providing water for the remaining feral livestock and wildlife that had survived the slash-burn. The cataloguing, the recording, and the investigation—well, that was all part of it too. But since the process-end, any academic funding was dependent on a provable experience-based approach to theory. After months and years of the trauma of slash-burn, folk had slowly woken up from the trance of thinking without doing. This, at least, was how it was seen. The basic argument was around form and shape—a holy awakening. It was both illegal and profane to preach Anarcho-primitivism, for example, whilst living on-grid and flying the few planet shuttles that remained from Upper New York to the Evangelical Republic of Africa. Human presence on Earth, aside from the old pre-proc locos off-grid, was mostly made up of miners and loggers and terraformers, and ideologically these pre- and post-process humans were not close at all. Everybody else was waiting to leave. Fale heard tales of unfound off-grid folk still somewhere, but surely, they could not last long, or be very well. What now for that counter ideal to technological advance, a dreamed-of *wild nature*? The Earth was ravaged. Technology was crucial as a means to survive Earth's atmosphere. 'Wildness is that which is not controlled by organized society,' wrote one old idiot.[16] There was a time when his voice became popular again and was co-opted by groups like the *ILF* and others. Most could not listen to his voice as he had admitted to killing people for his cause, which was understandable. It is an ugly thing to do. But the words of the idea could easily be repurposed. Pre-process, things were either right, or they were wrong. There was a primal way to this. Everybody was killing for causes, officially and unofficially. Who knew if those purported lost-wild locos living off-grid in the here and now—not that Fale thought they could be—were rather in a state of permanent celebration? Blood and soil, they used to say. *You want to do it like this*. All those fuckers destroyed in the slash-burn, leaving just the perfect little ethno-state somewhere out there in their enclosed wilderness, couples in Viking horns and braids singing about ethnic nationalism, eating from pork grids, and hunting wolves.

Fale turned back to the script he had received on his grab-phone. Should he report it to the university chancellors? There were certain videos—cock-worship, tongue-out, hairless-asshole, I-love-you-now-fuck— on his grab-phone that he would never share with anybody, they were so sexy and personal, when they had been as thick as thieves. But now this note out of the blue. What was he thinking? On the day he left, he was still banging on about utopias, top of the list being a kind of queer utopia where every-queer lived off the land and fucked who they wanted. But much time had passed. Utopias turned into kingdoms quite quickly, and there were few folks more likely to head up a rainbow ethno-state than him. That section on his degrees was clearly exaggerated. Even if he had passed the module on anti-greenwashing, he only ever paid lip service to living the anarcho-primitivist lifestyle, and in fact travelled extensively, shopped liberally, and gave talks internationally. He rarely stopped talking—teaching, he called it, or "exchanging." Just the kind of behaviour the new universities abhorred, basically—doing very little, in practice, but moving his mouth about with enormous eloquence. It was a mouth as deep as a cave. Fale remembered pissing in it and shifted. The cock-lord that broke all the rules. The boys loved him, which is where Fale came in. Anyway.

Now he had written a manifesto, and Fale shuddered at the script as it shone out of his grab-phone. Fale knew he could not report it to the chancellors. He flipped his phone shut and started through the acid showers. Soon he had on his vac mask and was headed back out to the toxic soil of the highest peaks.

The shuttle journey was short. With his globe-suit bunched up as always—who designed these fuckers?—he set off on the mountain road up to the old sunken hamlet, the ivy quadrant. Once it had been a dirt path, and the intern's great-great-great-great-grandfather, who had been a doctor, had reached the village on horseback. He had reached twenty different villages in every season under all weathers on horseback. Before that it had been a way of pilgrimage, and each of the peaks had a chapel—before that, a standing stone. The shaman hollered and screamed at the base of the huge menhir, asking the sky questions it would never answer. Later, for twenty years, it had been tarmacked over, and huge stones heaved into corners and edges to keep the gravel and cement in place. Only one of those workers thought about the stones' previous incarnation, which set his workmates cackling as they stood together at the site. After those twenty years had passed, the road had to be replaced. It was cracked and the winter storms had done their work. Pay cheap, pay twice, Fale's brother used to say. Farmers flew up the road on their jalopies, scattering wild and domestic animals in their wake and killing many. The *ILF Family Network (ILFFN)* lined the new road with pre-proc-end slogans, a billboard project on which many academic theses had since been written. *Important Love Fondu*, thought Fale. One of these billboards, investigating the *ILFFN* slogan "Action is Eloquence" (which itself was cribbed, arguably unknowingly, from *the* Shakespeare— the tremulous Bard who, as everyone now believed religiously, represented the pre-process technique of fucking an idea into submission), had become notorious as a basis for the post-proc New Shape Thinking and corresponding thinktanks, think-pieces and thought experiments. Only a few outliers saw that the post-proc ideology was modelled, perversely, on its predecessor.

During the belittlement measures of those terrible years before the process end, the slogan boards wilted into the fields beside the road; the fields became overgrown or were burnt in fires set by warriors and fools; the road, left to its own devices, began to return to dirt, sprouting marvellous weeds and dramatic cracks; and, finally, time continued to happen. When Fale reached the mastiff skull, he stopped under the pink and purple hazy. This was indeed a treasure. What if I were to stand here, holding the skull to the pink sky, and—alas!—speak to it? You may call this *failed entertainment.*[17]

CHAPTER 22: THE END OF PSYCHIATRY[18]

She was invisible in the wolf-night. She and her sisters killed the she-boar quickly, causing little pain. We are not the wolves who come in dreams. We are not the metaphors used by men, she would repeat. Repetition, the wolf knew, was a way of aligning. By day, the wolves were hidden. Watching. Wary of the humans who had spent a few thousand years befriending or killing her kind. Not that fucking surprising, right? There was a time when there had been so few wolves left—only six or seven, they said—that it seemed to be the end. Every way that they could find to kill wolves, they took. Poison in meat near their lairs or along their wolf-ways. Humans with large dogs and ever more accurate and destructive weapons. Wolf cubs, blocked up in dens and left to starve. The humans were affected by worshipful love or hatred and left it wherever they passed. There was a need to dominate the image of the wolf in humans so strong that it went far beyond the usual survival instinct a wolf might understand. It was impractical. For all the wolf knew, the humans did not realise their own luck, or other basic tenets. Whatever settled in their wake felt emotional and careless.

She called to her sisters. Something smelled wrong. At least two members of her pack were not present. Are they close? Soon, down through the crab apple and tiny oak, she found that they had been killed, beheaded—and then hanged from a yew tree, a horrible act so unholy as to taunt her. She bowed before the yew, praised the tree as friend, as gallows, and moved on. It was not the time to mourn. Nonetheless, that fucked things. *Good-work* would be impossible now—the surviving pack would not bring down the food they needed to feed every wolf and move forward into the next night with energy to feed again. They would have to do what she called *half-work*, which was to move down mountain to where humans pastured herds of horses and cows and swipe a young calf or foal. Easier pickings. But it became only *half-work* as it caused the humans to enact revenge more quickly. Covert hunters, with something hot, or unfamiliar, under their skins, roamed the mountains as zombies, feeling the kill but not honouring it fully. These zombies, the wolf supposed, had very little patience on a cellular level; and, within those cells, it would be impossible to find the receptors required to communicate, for example, with the yew tree. Now here she was, with only four or five wolves left in her hunting pack. Let the dead not be in vain. There had been great triumph in finding a small, overgrown path, with her pack, which wound into the dreams of some human, years ago, although she was not fully aware of how it had shaped the history of ideas. The journey had been very easy. Just left at the little woman peak, then straight for some miles. The appearance of certain animals or objects in human dreams gave factual meaning to certain ailments or fears that affected human movements and activities. She had ascertained this quickly. Then she set herself for play. For millennia the wolf and her ancestors had entered the dreams of humans at night as easily as they had slipped through the mountain pass after the bear. Humans were stubborn. Killing wolves in packs meant more lone wolves, and more *half-work*.

She padded her way into the dream of a little human with a big house. The dream was already quite busy. An old human narrated tales about the wolf and her sisters as if they were only stories and never real, weaving a spell about fathers and sisters and mothers and brothers. The dream was so obsessed with meaning the wolf felt quite suffocated. The human whose dream she inhabited seemed, within the dream at least, to accept that the narrator was extremely real, and the wolves were not. How much they seemed to know. The she-wolf found her way to the narrator and bit his dick. Stop it, fool, she growled. The narrator looked down at her and wrote some words in his notebook. He then moved over to the subject-human and explained to him some information about his sexual activity that, somehow, was related to the spell he had woven about family. The subject-human replied: the wolf is our madness, our ancient enemy, our talisman, our fear. The narrator shook his head and then nodded. The wolf was not surprised. Difficult for these humans, who lived dreams separately from waking. The wolf started to make her way gently, stealthily, backwards out of the dream, called to her remaining sisters, and moved up into the skull of the mountain.

I suggest you put the dream to good use. It was *winter in my dream, and night-time*, the man in the dream had said. He walked high up into the mountain plateau, beyond the peak of crows to the land they named after, he thought, the alpine oaks, although there were only hawthorns there now, and the shepherd's huts of stone were caved in. The man and his dogs had to go stone by stone, between the peak of the crows and the little woman, by way of an old drover's path, just stones heaved to the right or left. The upper mountain, made of limestone, was white and curved into angular shapes: flying buttresses, navel hollows, razor-clam burrows, raised fists. The mastiff always forged ahead first, only his long tail above the rocky outcrops and the rat dog at the man's side or just ahead. At the foot of a cave, long used to shelter cows, horses, goats and sheep from night-time wolf packs, was a copse of hazel and holly. The big mastiff was already through, while the little one, and the man, were singing the song of the bear. The song of the bear was a nonsense song to ward off the bear if she was resting in the copse. The words came from a dream, so they were real. The bear was real. Once, the bear had appeared before the man, risen on to her hind legs—heard the man tut disapprovingly— and run away into the woodlands. But most days, the man and his dogs were looking for the seventh wolf. The Wolf Man, the shapeshifter. The man kept on the mountain path. They went round the curtain of rock and up through the steep gully to the top. The seventh wolf, it seemed, was in the secret valley behind. Quickly they forged down the other side into the valley, the mastiff up ahead shouting now, the mongrel quick and suddenly leaping over gorse. It was exhilarating. The path was not clear here, how must the shepherds have taken their flocks down to the little lake below them? They pushed down to the high tarn. After the lake, which was shored up with a low stone wall, they climbed towards the highest peak. They chanted

Holly long claw arm,
oak mould leaves broke,
yew rock spell earth,
the kill of the wolf

three times, turning hare-wise round the peak until a chamois suddenly appeared, bold and unafraid. The mastiff barked, but the two must have had some kind of understanding because they did not address each other otherwise. I have seen the seventh wolf, said the chamois. He was standing with a pickaxe, his body lined with dazzling sun, so intense the man could hardly see his smile, but he was beautiful to him. The man suddenly remembered his picnic. He took out bread, brought this morning from the lady who drove at nine-thirty up the mountain to deliver bread to the little cabins that dotted the mountainside, their orbs open in the morning sun. She got to his village at nine-thirty, and the leftover bread the man used as treats for the dogs when it had dried and gone hard. Cheese. A thermos of coffee. A tomato. The dogs crowded around him. He felt that nothing was wrong with him. He thought nothing. But sometimes of course there was something. Sadness, panic, fear. He read once that a most interesting aspect of psychosis—perhaps theoretically—was the tendency to define things in a singular way. Or to know of hidden things that could never be found. *You should pay attention to your dreams.*

CHAPTER 23: BELITTLEMENT/THE PROCESS

Soon, the data-transfixed urban spaces were so profoundly caught up in personal battles against virtual, or artificial, thought processes, that conjecture was always under pressure of being belittled. Opinion was problematic, sanity or madness. People's voices were tuned by robots to sound more convincing—robotic wild sounds were the closest thing to their nature the city folk had. Separate tribes were warlike and precisely named, but they did nothing, only wrote, and wrote, and wrote, and responded "yes" (or "no") to other people's writing. Those who had the time to open up their ideas and turn them around tended to hide out or find employment with the king-makers. Linear time was such a precious commodity that the wealthy often held it in greedy reserve. This time, in turn, was configured through data, wherein it became much shorter and faster. Data-users lived in a tiny world and their languages were contemptuous. Who is being let out, and who is being let in, they shouted. And what is coming in and going out? Mobility of the wrong type was belittled. Wrong information of any type was treated with contempt or obsession. This is how the process started. This is what the history files say. We say the arc of stone has fallen at the mouth of the valley.

A gentle breeze rippled through the hazel that bordered his garden. Three new visitors had arrived, to help the little dog with his campaign against the rats. When they first came, from a teeming mass of cats a few villages over, they had been impossible to distinguish—three ginger kitten siblings. They must all be male, said the folk who passed by the cabin, the liquid crystal displays in their eye sockets bright with authority. They must live outside, said others. They must not be castrated, went one story; they must be castrated, went another. At all times their liquid crystal displays were dazzlingly convincing. The man wished for the orb to close over into its plinths and become whole again. So many ideas spoken with the air of veracity! But the kittens soon knew their place. The man spent weeks slowly introducing the little dog to his new brethren. At first, the little ratter went for them like he went for the barn rats, and the village cat they called Stain. Makes sense, dog, said the man. But wait a moment. The dog darted at them, and the man corrected him. The little cats shot into corners, into the crook of the man's neck, under the bed, up curtains. The man saw that two of them were twins, both female, and one was male. The tomcat was a richer burnt colour than the rest, striped like a tiger. The twins were paler, and one grew increasingly paler than her sister, ghost-like. At first, the mastiff growled and jumped as they leapt around him, but soon all five beasts were sharing space. The tomcat and the little rat dog slept together, curled up in ecstasy.

The man piled the three small cats into the jalopy, locked the dogs into the cabin precinct, and trundled down the mountain to find the animal doctor. Now the process had begun, everything was different—although for the man nothing much had changed. Folk were wide-eyed with, and hard-wired for, the expectation of disaster, and consumed tons of data to distract themselves from the end that they were convinced was coming, but that they couldn't see directly. The end was object—of derision, of reverence, of denial, of new beginnings. The man found, beyond this endless object, that love and work were the same thing, and the parallax of disaster, under these conditions, became less all-consuming. Even when the wolves entered dreams with explanations, these sleepy messages were widely diagnosed as anxiety caused by the process. The animal doctor's doors were still open, nonetheless. Gelt was more important now than ever. Fair enough. Folk desired it, even if only to get more data. Where there's data, there's gelt. The animal doctor exuded kindness, and cooed over the three little cats. Still blocked over at the fallen arc, right? That's right, she said. I'm still getting supplies through, but who knows how long for. Seems like the *ILF* will get their way. For now, all is the same. My purpose is clear. These little ones. Not much else. The man nodded. You leave these three with me, in a couple of hours they'll be capped and ready to go home. The man walked out into the street, and a bell sounded as he closed the door behind him. Where was the dog who walked the main street grinning and showing his teeth, chattering fuckers, fuckers, fuckers? He's dead, came a voice, he was knocked down by a jalopy. Should have jumped the other way. The voice cackled. Ah, poor little guy, answered the man. You'll be next, you big, spliced pig, the voice replied, chuckling. The man looked around for a set of liquid crystal displays. Nothing. Outside the tobacco shop, a huge sign advertising data dwarfed the signs for cigarettes ("we've got non-nicotine dummy-cigs for babies, too!"), the woman's publicity for the *ILFFN* ("You want to do it like this!"), the tiny bar with cobbled floors ("drinking, data & derring-do"), and the spliced pig tree plantations ("A spliced pig is a happy pig"). The horses giggled nervously at the gate. Vultures flew overhead, and drones with tuned voices: "Sustainability! Nature! The ethno-state!" This was the way of the process.

With more time to kill, he rode his jalopy slow up

past the donkey barns and over to the plantations. He waved at the two men as they fondled their donkeys' ears and removed droppings from the field. They looked sullen, and the man was sure one of them looked towards the barn, and then quickly, secretly away. Fear not, brothers, he said under his breath. I am with you. We all have something hidden in our souls. He halted at the plantation gate, whose massive data-filled sign, advertising all manner of pork products, pointed the way to rows and rows of shifting, pulsating trees into the distance. To the left of the entrance, the recently-finished visitor centre was colourful with signs about god's creation of the pig, god's contemporaneous creation of the tree, something about pigs and trees that had been transferred from the holy book and passed under a scientific lens, and finally the godly reason for the union of spliced pig trees, which was fundamentally linked to human survival, superiority and some weirdness about god's pig on a tree and pigtrees as god's children. The man laughed, but his eyes were wide. *Icky Loyal Foot-soldiers.* The trees themselves had no real relation to the earth—their "trunks" were dug into soil, or drilled into rock, to give them stability and wait for synth fertiliser. This trunk in its upper reaches then formed the backside and body-shape of a pig, and the tip, or head, of the tree was comprised of pig-like snout, ears, and liquid crystal displays. These latter displays were both aesthetic, to make the spliced pig tree live up to its name and publicised image, but also mechanical, as they absorbed the sun's energy and helped the pig develop its meat. Solar powered pig. Beside the visitor's centre and the unfinished tech hub, disguised with timber cladding and dug into the earth so as not to appear so palatial, were the series of slaughterhouses where the plucked pig trees were sent to be processed. They were heavily insulated and connected to the acres of pig trees by tracks that criss-crossed the lots. Around the place the man could see pig trees being plucked from the ground, inseparable until death, an activity which was mostly shielded from view by tarps or machinery. The man could hear the squeals and cries of the spliced pig trees as the workers ripped them from their holes in the ground, loaded them into transport, and quickly replaced them with a tiny sapling with an unformed, wailing pig head at its tip. Finally, at one far corner of the plot a huge bonfire smoked continuously, filling the sky with acrid smoke. What a fucking place, thought the man. The more the process became apparent, the more spliced pig plantations became urgently necessary. Near half the world ate pork, and those that didn't ate chicken. That was just the way it was.

He cantered back from the plantations to the animal doctor. The horses gathered, worried, at the gate as he passed. Three sleepy cats lay prostrate in the doctor's surgery. The tomcat was stirring and looked up drunkenly. All fine, the animal doctor said. Those girls will need watching. Cut a sock and pull it over their bodies to cover their wounds. Give the tom a few hours and he's good to go. That'll be a thousand in gelt. The man counted out his money, loaded the little cats up onto his jalopy and turned for the skull of the mountain. Come on you three, he whispered. Time to cure those wounds and get to work. Rat dog needs your help. The kittens lolled on their cushion, hardly awake.

CHAPTER 24:
CONVERSATION

The man woke up from his nap with a start. The tiger-striped tomcat was plugged against his lower stomach, and the twins clasped together behind the crook of his knee, one pale, one marked. The mastiff was flat out on the floor, and the little mongrel was curled up under his bed. The wolves, four or five of them now, were a way across the mountain. There is work to be done, said the man.

He had spent months cutting back and collecting different-sized lumps of wood, of different types. He did this every year. The near wall of the barn was a series of log-piles which the man knew intimately and whose order he recognised. The first pile was ash wood, first to be burnt, if necessary and the cold weather came quick, or late—ash could be burnt green, on a bad day. Then hawthorn, which had grown out of control down the bottom field, started off as a pile of wild- and weird-shaped thinnish trunks and small logs, many with huge spikes on the lesser branches. Little by little the rich ruby wood was cut into manageable pieces which he could pile up. Any wood when it is sized and split looks neat and finds its place in the pile, however impossible or unruly the situation in the wild. There was a time when the man thought he could do everything by hand. He dreamed he would scythe the grasses and saw the trees, sweating like an ancestor. After one year on the land, he started working very hard to make gelt so that this would not be so. By the second year he had two chainsaws for smaller and larger trees. This was better. The third pile was oak, a tree which appeared as saplings very quickly each spring and as years passed, formed woodland on un-stewarded land. This tree should be split as soon as the large chunks had been jalopied and dragged back to the barn, because it was sappy inside and needed air to breathe. He spent many months admiring these log-piles during the spring, summer, and early autumn months, making sure they were airing and curing well—until his body hit a certain temperature, his indoor coat no longer did its job, and he lit the first fire of the autumn. This was always a happy ceremony, and each stick was known personally to him. Out in the field, every tree that he cleared out of its space was replaced with a new one elsewhere, or one sprung up. Since many years before the process, the mountain had been left to turn wild, so there was a great deal of fallen wood and small trees to clear and collect. Many called this Nature, and celebrated its wildness, came by shuttle to see it, even. But it was, in effect, like all the planet, either pre- or post-industrial. With pigs mostly replaced by spliced pig trees, only the wild boar, deer and other wild creatures were left to clear the woodland and, roaming free as they did, could not be relied on to clean the forest floor as thoroughly as domesticated pigs.

When today's work on the woodpile was finished, the next job should begin. The sun glinted on the casings of the retractable house-orb. A helicopter whirred in the distance. There were glazed eyes glinting back at him from behind glass in the windows of nearby cabins. Soon, they would all be gone for winter, corralled into their data channels in the city, happier there despite the terrible decay and constant post-war rebuilding. The man moved past the barn to the kitchen garden and put on a pair of gloves. He walked round, dogs and cats at his feet, pulling out nettles at the roots from their pernicious homes in cracks and corners and lining the vegetable beds. When he had a fair pile of them, and impossibly stung hands despite the gloves, he pushed them all into a bucket and covered them with water. In a few weeks he'd have fertiliser for the newest plants—the smelliest, nitrogen-richest potion in the garden. Soon it would be time to cut back the hedgerows. They were filled with rose-hip, bramble and dog rose, leaning over his field like spies. Or tall with hazel, which would be handy for weaving and strengthening fences come the cold months. He walked further down the field with a shovel in his hand, reaching the three little water holes he had dug in the soil above the limestone. He cleared debris, mud and leaves out of each one and waited for the water to clear. Bees and other insects hovered where the water seeped out of the rock or soil. One swam where he had accidentally knocked it in, then wrenched itself out, buzzing angrily. The cats sipped delicately at the edge, so did the mongrel. As always, the mastiff came, scattered animals and insects, and plunged his feet deep into the muddy water, drinking his fill, slurping noisily for minutes. There would be fuel, food and water, the man said to himself. He understood to think twice when it seemed there was radical change. In one lifetime, change could be so slow as to appear almost unrecognisable. The things that happened fast in a time of global belittlement were not the radical changes. The man listened to the fluty sounds of the shaman, high in the karst system, but when he listened for his friend in the cave heard only a shining silence.

Over the next few months, the cats bought him the following kills, dropping them at his feet, or taking them into the spare room and ripping them apart: yellow finches; chickadees; dunnocks; blackbirds (male and female); magpie chicks (magpies screamed around the house for days, dive-bombing the cats, dogs, and the man); many lizards of all sizes; slow worms; moles; mice; and, rats. When the time came to clean under the spare bed, the man discovered piles of sticky, melting bodies, headless victims, and discarded organs. The village cats, including the one they called Stain, circled the house looking for war, and the man sent the dogs flying at them. The palest cat spoke in little bursts, her voice tentative and urgent. Her sister only spoke when she needed to eat but was polite about it. The tomcat woke up shouting, wailed and chattered through the day, and fell asleep telling himself long stories of derring-do, only to wake up in the middle of the night to continue the conversation. Famously, a leader adjacent to the king-makers had publicly stated, especially concerning the ethics of spliced pig trees, that "if people come to me with stories about talking animals, they're probably not my kind of people" to great acclaim. The man knew different. Quite fucking right, piped up the tomcat.

CHAPTER 25: LAND MANAGEMENT

She stood up, her highlighted hair and heavy jewellery bright in the glare of the strip-light of the visitor centre, her three phones on a chain around her neck. On the dais in front of her, she carried data patches, legal data highs, data bribes, up-data, and algorithm hacks. Well, here we go, she thought. I'm nervous. But her riches were all around her. I'm the queen of this beehive, she told herself. Welcome friends, she started. Here to keep our land and families our own. Our own, owned by us, worked by us, and enjoyed by us. Keeping it rural! Keeping it wild! She held her fingers in the *ILF* salute, the palm representing the trunk of a tree, and two skyward fingers of processed pig. Her audience responded. Hot masculine dads and cool feminine mums; well-dressed lady-like grannies and twinkly-eyed manly grandads; braces of cisgender kids—at least three per family, but two of each pleased many; the odd bachelor; one or two spinsters; these last three types were treated as people on their way to lifelong union with one other person of complementing gender expression. Thanks for coming to the site of our national pig trees! Wild philosophy, ethnicity, and progress! God with you all. May the arc enclose us. Tonight's talk is about conspiracies, of which there are many and which I am trained up on and moved to explain to you. My emotions are running high, so you will excuse me, but at least, as you know me, and we are friends, what I say, through the tears, is true. Remember, and let's say this together, "You want to do it like *this*!"

Firstly, and these are not the worst, believe me, are the things we have been told about the so-called process. There *is* a plague virus! There *is* a data virus! Denying this is a way for them to hide from us who is coming in, and who is leaving—and conceal the fact that things don't come in or out anymore. The true conspiracy is the anti-ethno-state pig-porkers—those rich perverted people in suits who steal our pig trees, feed our children to them, and then force themselves sexually into the pigs, little pig trees with food bellies that reveal *our children inside*! We should be keeping our Pig Grid market safe—and full o' pork! Sure, the supermarkets have got empty shelves, but nothing gets in or out these days. We'll stock our own shelves, like our grandfathers always could. Keep it local. Some are against nostalgia, but I say the future is in the past. Nobody is outsourcing my survival to a distant hub. Then they say our rewilded pig plantations are fire hazards, full of sickness. This honeycomb logic! These words from the ivory tower! How do you feel, my friend? She pointed to the well-dressed farmer-dad to her left. Why, I feel strong as a boar, smiled the man. Sure as heaven you do! And they want to centralise our pig grids? Not on my watch! It's only a matter of time before everyone bleeds from their mouth or their ears. Have you? Nobody said yes. We want to live—we need business, and we've got all the information at our fingertips, the truth of how to rewild the land, god be praised. We need gelt, the pig grids bring it. We need to eat, and we've got a valley full of pork fields. We need to go back to the city and get good data—nobody is curtailing my right to travel wherever I want—but the arc might be down forever, and heavens we'll control who gets in and who gets out. Meanwhile, look at all these great jalopies that roll over the rock like tanks. Our jalopies. We need to work together, because that way our people, ones like us, get stronger. As for this conspiracy about data—good data is good data, and my algorithm is under control, it makes me feel… she stopped. Her eyes were shining… it makes me feel safe. I want to feel safe, don't you? She looked across at the cool feminine mums and the lady-like grannies. Don't you? They nodded nervously, checking their phones. When I say safety, I mean safe from illegals who do not belong on the land, land that we have inherited from our forefathers who knew about sustainability before it was even a word. Those who do not have strong data intelligence—*truth*—can go rewild elsewhere. How else am I going to get home with bags filled o' pork? The audience laughed good-naturedly. Later, when the *ILF* had created one of the early self-contained, ethno-states of the process, and the valley was bristling with armed militia patrolling the sustainable spliced pig tree plantations, she would often look into the mirror and say to herself tremulously: remember, all the things they say, they are lies. She had never had a strong sense of what was entering her body and what was leaving it. She was afraid. When the people started dying, bleeding from various body holes, it seemed not to be the fault of the pig grids. Even before the slash-burn, her sickly daughter would use that mirror to tell herself things that sounded as profoundly true as the teeth that fell from her mouth.

Secondly, and this has been brought to my attention quite recently, the data says there are some wild folk out there using, taking, and even soiling our land—and, I'm afraid, fucking our pig trees. I'm not talking about those two fruits at the donkey barns, I've said to them time and time again, I do not care what you do at home as long as you don't rub it in our faces. If you behave like a dad or a mum—and by that, I mean an expressively original human with normal behaviours—you're following the rules. Donkeys aren't human kids though, and you know that. Don't get me started on the topic of "fur babies." But there were some dangerous folk after the war, up in the caves, and I've heard they're endangering the lifestyle of our children and potentially infecting the data supply on a national level. Different folk who desecrate the family unit. Neither men nor women. Something in between. And flaunting it! This will lead to a global data outage. It's black or white. If the process means anything at all—which I am not sure it does—it means cleansing, through ethnic and sexual health, and proper land management. We want pig farmers—but only the ones who know what family is! We want pigs—but only the ones that grow on trees! The audience broke out into stuttering laughter. I say to you all, and I will say it again—I've got nothing against things you do in your own home, but if my kids are in danger—I will get my gun! If my data is going to get infected through perverted acts, well, I'll get my other gun, and double-fist. I'll hunt them like wolves. There are people out there who do not understand the truth in my voice, and they are the ones to hunt. Watch out for weirdos and perverts. There are a few here on the wrong side of the arc that we'll soon weed out. Keep your eyes peeled. Protect our kids! Protect our data! Protect our pig trees! Protect our land! With each jubilant statement she emphasised the word "protect," rolling the *r* for as long as she could. A child in the middle of the audience put his hand up, and she smiled towards him. Yes, my love, and isn't god good? Yes, god is good, and thank-you for the extra data you've been sending to our private school (not the public one). Pig grid money paid for that, she said. His crystalline eyes holes lit up. My question is, what do we do when we find out, even in real life, that a kid is different from the rest, alone or unclear, one who doesn't care about their future family? His friends sniggered. Mind your backs, she laughed. No, but seriously, these are sad kids that need help. Report them, and they'll get picked up, diagnosed, and cured—men are masculine, and women are feminine, there is no doubt—and you've no idea how revolutionary the modern world of psychiatry is, my child. Those kids have got wolves in their minds, bad wolves. Thanks for the question—here! And she threw him more data packs. His liquid crystal displays glazed in triumph. He and his friends fell on the data, pinged it to their phones and floated away blissfully into a virtual place of wolf hunting and, later, choke-fucking, hairless-holing, and other private, disallowed gaming. You want to do it like *this*.

Outside, the sky was alive with song beyond the pig grids. The bear pulled berries off the trees at the edge of the mountain pasture. The man pushed tiny cauliflower seedlings into the ground in his garden. The giant readied their limestones, poised on the mountain peak. Please thank us, sang the trees. And the wolf—well, she sang what she heard in dreams:

menamenanwiminawimin
menamenanwiminawimin
menamenanwiminawimin
menamenanwiminawimin
menamenanwiminawimin
menamenanwiminawimin
menamenanwiminawimi
menamenanwiminawiminoooooooooooooooooo

CHAPTER 26: THE SEVENTH WOLF[19]

I do not count time. I am not free; the land is my steward. The adder does not have as much venom in its tail as a human tongue. When the wasp bites, the hand can balloon to five times its natural size, and the venom may creep up the arm. After two days, it reaches the throat. Hand to arm shaped like a spade. I am half-man, half-mole, the man rejoiced, to nobody in particular. The land shifted my shape, before the end. It's garlen, lads. What fucking end, barked the mastiff. You're here, aren't you? The moons keep doing those circles you bang on about. Up there, painted on that big ol' black canvas I roar up to when the orb has whirred shut. Where the seventh wolf is painted on a sky of green-grey, and lopes forward, away from you, head down. The man laughed, winced in pain, and then jumped. The dogs were barking. Oi! The hippy poked his crystal eyes through the fence: alright, outsider? What you doing? Long time no see, answered the man. I'm running out of money, might have to exchange my wife for a couple of donkeys, said the hippy. I'm sure she'd love that, replied the man good-naturedly, those were the days when you could sell your wife for a herd of donkeys—not! Actually, replied the hippy, warming to his own authority, it was more like a dowry, if we're being strictly historical—you want do it like *this*, as they say! The man had no words. He slipped the hippy some gelt and the little bearded elf sauntered away. Watch out for those wolves coming off the mountain, they'll take your chickens, shouted the hippy, and those wolves at the *ILF*, don't even get me started, he cackled. The man called after him: what if the wolf is just a creature, running out of frame? But the hippy had gone, and the man's question hung in the air. *My open eye, to the light—move to the shadow, wait for it, wait for the night—wait for the light in the night.* The mongrel growled. I miss that weird dog, the one that used to gabble fucker, fucker, fucker. We used to go by his place, me, and tiger mastiff, and the three of us would prance up through the heather to make the cows and horses shift around like molasses, before the farmers came in their jalopies and took pot shots at us. Good times. Those little humble loves and infinite jests. The first time the wolf and her pack entered his dreams, the man was fucked up on data deep in the city, just after the war. Now he thought about it, war had always just been around the corner. The great king-maker in the sky was always watching and plotting, had been eyeing us all up, me since I was a kid stealing women's skins from the back corner of the shaman's cave before the deep drop into beyond. Fonsu, the dark wren from the far northern woods, told me of his sense of being always watched. It might be in my head, he would tell me, as we strolled through the aftermath. The wolf smiled, somewhat voraciously, and Fonsu looked about him. Fear. I've always been scared, really, and that is what a war footing does—turn the corner and they'll get you. Always vigilant. Hyper vigilant. How can you avoid the end if you're not vigilant? The wolf looked me in the eyes and said, this is what you idiots call a dream.

The man rarely stepped foot in the city. He told himself that he did not need data. He could go without it for months, years even. Then suddenly one day he'd up-data two thousand in gelt and get messaging and feeling and finding and rising and moving and surfing and then towards the end of his data maybe charge his liquid crystal displays to the pornheart and fuck an uncle and his pig grid farmer friend in a Real so well configured his cum arcs up and is lost in the skull of the mountain, miles beyond the cabin's orb. There is nothing more real, after all, than heavy data dreams. Or, to put it more clearly, who is not curious about what is getting in and what is coming out? Meanwhile, the road ended quite abruptly at the billboards before the cabins. Fale, in his globe-suit, photographed the colours of the leaves and measured the toxicity of the aftermath. Would he ever get a globe-suit that just fit perfectly? Or perhaps that was asking too much. He looked up to the sky and sang his own wolf-song to the departing star cruisers:

The dewdrop sacrals. The chronicles kept
In their glass vials, sealed flood container.
The pilgrims dream of rules that flesh
Might follow if liquid is almost a shape.

Water collects at the nape of the neck.

Our world revolving, a skull, a jewel now.
Tiny garden pools hid in the mountains,
Bands of warriors ready in karst caves.
There is water embedded in your forehead.

The cruisers moving in the hopeful dark

With their seas & rivers in laboratories,
Mer-clones programmed with tales
Of sea-lovers lost, the kind whale who
Grows the algae & washes the dishes.

They bought their silver suits online

To be wrapped in. I remember when

A narwhal told me, child, the unicorn
Of the sea only *looks* worth saving -
The beauty of anything lit by suns.

Well, shit. I am a sunbeam myself.

The star fire that we roved through,
Past the waterfall in its first trimester.
Tell me, queer ancestors & hawthorn
Trees & magic stones, what to do

With our granite n' metal psyches?

Is that gurgling-around your voice,
Is it is it is it is it?

Is that shudder behind your eyelids
- the breath of the sphere -
a store of liquid?
Is it is it is it is it?

Is that wolf, the one in dreams,
Your purpose?
It is it is it is it is

You sing out of tune, said the man. The dogs howled.
There's work to do, those fields do not clear themselves.

He shrugged on his skins, reached for a spade. He was no longer formless. Now, from the beginning of the song, through the squally chorus of dogs whining, he was attuned to a gap in time where moments existed that he could not quite grasp. Still, light was in the night of his forgetfulness and harmlessly traced an outline around his body. There was a helicopter overhead. Soon enough, on wolf-night, the cabin would be surrounded. Trees, wolves, anything that could enter a dream and leave at will. Everything would be bristling.

A QUEER NETWORK

Songs by Roísín Murphy, Deee-lite, Kate Bush, Tracy Chapman, Dolly Parton and Me'shell Ndegeocello echo across the times of the story, alongside other such affinities:

1   'Tape 2: The Earth' by Edwin Morgan, in *New Selected Poems* (Carcanet, 2000).

2   The words in italics in these paragraphs are misheard from songs by the band Joy Division.

3   This information was inspired by unforgotten recorded events in northern rural Spain during the Spanish Civil War, especially the oral account of Enésida García Suárez (1926-2001) in *Mi Infancia en el Franquismo* (Tiraña, Asturies, 1938), (Camabalache: Oviedo, 2018). The Association of relatives and friends of the mass grave at Tiraña came about in 2014 to continue the work of conserving the historical memory started by a group of relatives during the Francoist dictatorship, collectively memorialised at the Tiraña cemetery (Asturias, Spain) since 1977.

4   See *Cabezas en un paisaje (Heads in a Landscape)* from *Las Pinturas Negras (The Black Paintings)* (1819-1823), Francisco Goya

5   Spain's *pacto de olvido* (pact of forgetting) after Franco's dictatorship (1939-1975) is the model here.

6   Sigmund Freud´s patient Sergei Konstantinovich Pankejeff, who later became known as the Wolf Man, recounted this dream to his psychoanalyst. Famously, from this account, Freud created his own theories about what had happened.

7   Minnie Riperton's greatest hits.

8   My translation/version from the poem 'XIX', from *Por el camino de Swann* (1968), by Leopoldo Maria Panero (1948-2014).

9   See *Figure in a Landscape* (1945), Francis Bacon.

10   Jan Liwacz was a master blacksmith who was imprisoned in Auschwitz, and whose camp number was 1010. The SS ordered him to make the *Arbeit Macht Frei* sign. On the 6th May 1945 he trekked with his cell mate Alfons Wrona from the Mauthausen camp in Austria, to Poland (over 200 miles) where Liwacz worked as a smith. He died in 1980.

11   Thich Nhat Hanh, *The Miracle of Mindfulness*, translated by Mobi Ho (Beacon Press, 1975).

12   From Audre Lorde, 'The master's tools will never dismantle the master's house' (1979).

13   see the work of university professor David Vilaseca (1964-2010). Paul Julian Smith writes in Vilaseca's obituary in the UK newspaper *The Guardian*: "the Spanish novelist Juan Goytisolo came to identify himself as a homosexual only when told as much by his mentor, Jean Genet. This was a fine example of the "hindsight" of David's title, the way in which

retrospectively we build narratives of ourselves, telling tales that are never simple or single."

14 Maggie Nelson, *The Argonauts* (London: Melville Press, 2016)

15 Adapted from a flyer circulated by mystic/teacher George Gurdijeff for an early school in Georgia, 1919.

16 Theodore Kaczynski, 'Progress Versus Wilderness', Labadie Box 65, p. 2, citing Roderick Nash, 'The Future of Wilderness: The Need for a Philosophy', *Wild America* (July 1979), pp. 12—13, archived in the University of Montana's Clifton R. Merritt Papers, Box 110, Folder 2.

17 Which was, as you may know, a title David Foster Wallace had in mind for his novel *Infinite Jest* (1996)

18 Title borrowed from Leopoldo María Panero's prose-poem 'Acerca del caso Dreyfuss (sic) sin Zola o la causalidad diabólica/El fin de la psiquiatría'('On the Dreyfus case without Zola or diabolical causality/ The End of Psychiatry' (1987), in which Panero writes that "Every human being has the potential to be a psychiatrist, if he would just lend us his mirror." (my translation, in Leopoldo María Panero, *Poesía Completa* (1970-2000) (Visor, 2004).

19 See Francis Bacon, *Dog* (c.1967)

www.ingramcontent.com/pod-product-compliance
Lightning Source LLC
Chambersburg PA
CBHW031238260626
47169CB00007B/2359